6 Endearing Stories from Kashmir

Rubina Sushil

INDIA • SINGAPORE • MALAYSIA

Copyright © Rubina Sushil 2022
All Rights Reserved.

ISBN 979-8-88783-976-9

This book has been published with all efforts taken to make the material error-free after the consent of the author. However, the author and the publisher do not assume and hereby disclaim any liability to any party for any loss, damage, or disruption caused by errors or omissions, whether such errors or omissions result from negligence, accident, or any other cause.

While every effort has been made to avoid any mistake or omission, this publication is being sold on the condition and understanding that neither the author nor the publishers or printers would be liable in any manner to any person by reason of any mistake or omission in this publication or for any action taken or omitted to be taken or advice rendered or accepted on the basis of this work. For any defect in printing or binding the publishers will be liable only to replace the defective copy by another copy of this work then available.

For
Mummy & Daddy

About Rubina Sushil

Rubina is from Kashmir and so, holds all things Kashmiri close to her heart. Growing up in a close-knit society where every member, young as well as old, has a role to play, is enriching she admits. The warm association is extended far beyond families, and this is what makes Kashmiris unique. Her understanding of these special bonds between the people who live in this special universe of their own is expressed profoundly through her writing.

Rubina has worn many hats throughout her three-decade-old career. She has been associated with leading national newspapers, TV shows and magazines. As an entrepreneur, she successfully launched her own ventures: a preschool and day-care and a travel agency.

She has authored a coffee table book 'Under My Blue Sky,' which gives us a glimpse of Kashmir never seen before.

Contents

QUIVER 9

    Chapter 1   Jabbar Jigar 11

    Chapter 2   Maqsooda 37

DRIFTWOOD 43

    Chapter 1 45

    Chapter 2 52

    Chapter 3 55

    Chapter 4 58

SHADOW 61

    Chapter 1 63

    Chapter 2 66

    Chapter 3 71

    Chapter 4 75

    Chapter 5 80

    Chapter 6 85

PART 2 89

    Chapter 1 91

Contents

VOICE **97**

    'What Were You Doing?' 99

QUICKSAND **111**

    Chapter 1 113

    Chapter 2 120

    Chapter 3 137

    Chapter 4 146

STEEL **151**

PART 1 ....**153**

PART 2 ....**177**

PART 3 ....**181**

PART 4 ....**189**

Glossary *193*

QUIVER

Chapter 1

Jabbar Jigar

'*Mobile dekhna kya ha*i,' a giggle, a smirk and a high-pitched laugh were shared by three young ladies, sitting on bolsters at the corner of the huge, crowded tent. Hands with beautiful *henna* designs were desperately trying to keep the yellow 'designer' dupattas from slipping from heads that rocked to and fro as the subject of their gossip grew spicier and their laughter even more uncontrollable. The target of their diatribe was a lanky, tall, fair, slightly stubbled youngster, with dark eyes and long lashes. Dressed in a white *kurta-pyjam*a with gold buttons and a light blue waistcoat, he was standing nearby, pretending to be engrossed in his phone. But he could hear them clearly, even while the whole tent was a cacophony of the beats of several *tumbakhnaris*, the shrill singing of a lone guest, and hundreds of women laughing and talking excitedly. He looked up sharply, curled his upper lip and held out his hand to show off his new, shiny phone. 'Mobile *nahin,* iPhone 11 *hai,*' a husky, singsong voice told them off. If he thought this would shut them, he was mistaken. For the girls held their breath for a moment and together burst out in loud peals of laughter.

"*It was our destiny that we are not men, nor women. But to survive, we have to learn to live with them. There's nothing more or less to it. We live in two different worlds, my Jigar. Accept and live with it,*" Ayub Bab's words rang in Jabbar Jigar's ears, as always consoling him whenever he felt a hot lava of anger bubbling in his chest. Ayub Bab, his mother, father and friend rolled all in one, was the gentlest and wisest soul Jabbar had ever come across. Besides, he was used to these jibes and the looks of curiosity, amusement or sarcasm that often came his way.

Taking a deep breath, Jabbar calmly walked past the giggling trio, murmuring loudly enough to let them hear, 'Just wait. Very soon, I'm the one person you'll not want to mess with!'

The shocked girls covered their mouths with the back of their hands to stifle their loud shrieks, while an elderly lady sitting next to them glared at them and reprimanded them for teasing the poor *manzimuour*.

'Where are you? You were supposed to be here an hour back! I'm sure you have been going to the other wedding behind my back! Now, get your ass here as soon as possible or I'll kill your entire *khandaan*!' Jabbar barked at the phone.

By now, he was frothing at the mouth with anger. He was sure Sanam was running a parallel business behind his back. Sanam, whom he had known all his life to be the biggest liar he had met, was also his most loyal friend.

'Jigar, I swear on my mother's grave. I'm very much here, with the *waza*, helping with the *kehwa*.'

'You better be there, or I will skin you alive!'

"*If only Sanam could handle Fatimaji,*" he thought, nodding his head from side to side. The mother of the bride, Fatimaji, was one hell of a client to please. Loud and bossy, she held the remote control for every movement of the occupants of her household. Nothing escaped her ever-vigilant eyes. Her stout frame and flaming red hennaed hair together with those piercing blue eyes made most people buckle under easily. God forbid, no one wanted to be around her when she was angry! Nicknamed '*Byil*' or the blue-eyed one, she made people shudder with just a flick of an eye and an icy look. Jabbar didn't want to be the one to tell her that the guestlist of the ladies coming from the groom's side for tonight's *mehendi* ceremony had been doubled at the last minute. No amount of cajoling the groom's mother had worked.

"*What can I do?*" Gulshanlala had lamented. "*So many relatives are now upset with me,*" she had said with a distinct rattle in her voice. "*I had thought that the cousins from my side would at least understand and had left them out of the list. But today, there was a siege at my place, where my second cousin and her in-laws literally shouted at me for not finding them suitable enough for accompanying the rest of the girls to the bride's home. 'Is our presence going to lower your standards? Are we going there to eat the pastry? Saakib is our brother. Our daughters will regret this for their entire life that they were not allowed to go to the bride's place for the mehendi,'* they said *Jigara*," she had cried hysterically. "*These are the girls that Saaku has not even met before, but today, they are his sisters. I'm helpless! Balailagai, tell Fatimaji we are sorry.*" The picture of her holding her chin between her fingers in a gesture of pleading kept flashing in his mind. "*In any case,*" she had continued with a shrug of her shoulders and new found confidence, "*It's not much of an inconvenience. I'm sure they will manage with the khaatirdaari.*"

Sanam was nowhere to be found. He was not with the head *waza*, the one who fed him roasted liver on the sly, nor with the guy supplying the cold drinks. He rushed to the second floor of the huge house, which was being readied for the guests. The groom's relatives would be sitting in the hall the size of a football field. The finest Kashmiri wall-to-wall carpets were being laid out. The sheer white curtains complemented the dozens of large white bolsters and colourful embroidered cushions placed against the walls.

'Have you seen Sanam?' he asked Taufiq.

He felt a bout of anxiousness as Taufiq never lost a chance to tease him. He was one character who Jabbar disliked to the core. Taufiq was unrolling a 6X8-foot silk carpet on the left side of the room, where the bride would be sitting.

'Oh, Sanam, the one who is your sister, or brother, eh *aashiq*?' he giggled. Straightening himself he walked over to Jabbar. 'Look, I'm not into that kind of a thing,' he winked.

'Carry on. What can we do without you, Taufi dear,' Jabbar retorted sarcastically, nodding and turning his back abruptly so that he wouldn't have to catch the jeer in Taufiq's eyes.

He knew now that the onus was on him to break this news to Fatimaji. Wringing his hands, he thought of the difficult task ahead. As a *manzimuour*, the matchmaker, he had to act as a bridge between the bride and the groom's family. At first, he was rather tactless at this whole business, which mostly depended on how good one was at exaggeration. But with each alliance or a rejected one, he grew bolder. 'The boy reads the *namaz* five times a day, and never misses a fast during Ramadan.' 'The girl is innocent and shy. According to her neighbours, she has never been seen even glancing out of a window!' were the lies he had blatantly told. He had often regretted the decision of approaching Fatimaji for the alliance of her daughter. But the money was so alluring! The groom was from a very well-to-do business family, and though the couple was actually having a love marriage, the job was given to him to make it look like it was arranged.

The day Jabbar met Fatimaji for the first time, he knew he was in for a lot of trouble. From the very beginning, she had feigned ignorance of the affair between her daughter and the boy. 'Naazu hasn't ever stepped out of the house alone. Her brother even drops her for tuition class,' she had lied. 'No, I think we can't say yes to such a *rishta*. That guy must be meeting some other Naaz.' He had been literally thrown out of the house the next couple of times he approached her. She did finally come around, but not before announcing that this was strictly an arranged match and that her Naazu had never met the would-be-groom.

Fatimaji's hysterical reaction to anything that was beyond her control was legendary. And this was the wedding of her only daughter, the apple of her eye. She wanted all the functions to be memorable and had spent several sleepless nights going through all the minute details in her mind repeatedly. She had instructed her husband to write everything down in a 10-year-old unused diary which she dug out from the wooden almirah used for hoarding things – things she knew would one day come handy. The almirah – tucked under the wooden staircase at the entrance of the house – had a plethora of random items, either purchased but never used or received as gifts. These would be carefully stacked up and dusted from time to time. There was always something that could be useful in an emergency when you didn't have time to buy a gift. A garish purse that her mother-in-law had got her from haj, was dispatched off to a distant cousin whose husband had dropped in suddenly for dinner. The tea set that she purchased on impulse, the one with the gold edging, the one that her darling daughter Naaz had wanted to use on several occasions but wasn't allowed, well, finally had seen the light of the day when her sister-in-law came for *mubaarak* on Naazu's graduation. It was lying there as well, with the rest of the other things that weren't as lucky as the tea set.

As Jabbar passed the almirah that had a huge padlock on it, he saw the same lady who had been singing in the tent, coming out of the bathroom. Looking a little hassled, she waved at him, gesturing at him to come to her. He was in a tearing hurry now, as it was nearly 5 P.M and the *mehendi* party from the groom's side was likely to arrive in a couple of hours. He had to find Fatimaji and inform her about their changed plans.

'*Kath bozu*. Listen. Can you help me?' the lady was gesturing frantically at him.

He quickly went towards her, and immediately knew what she wanted from him. Holding one end of her *pista*-green dupatta, she handed over the other end to Jabbar.

'Why did you have to wash it?' he asked in an irritated voice.

'I spilt *nun chai*. It's a pure chiffon *dupatta*, it would have got ruined and the stain would never go if I hadn't washed it. You are the *manzimuour*, aren't you?' she asked rather shyly.

He was surprised at her shyness, for she was middle-aged and he mostly got a lot of attitude from ladies, having dealt with them on a daily basis. Their behaviour with him was always predictable. Caring and generous one day, arrogant and haughty the very next day. But this lady – plump, fair with light brown hair and pleasant features – was not mocking him; he was sure about that.

'Where can we dry it? There are people everywhere,' he asked. 'Quick, come inside the bathroom. I'll put the fan on full speed and you can help me dry it.'

A full five minutes later, the pretty lady, whose name he learnt was Maqsooda and who happened to be Fatimaji's best friend and neighbour, stepped out, her *dupatta* now firmly in place. She walked into Fatimaji's bedroom on the ground floor without knocking, with Jabbar in tow. The room was littered with baskets and trays overflowing with *mithai* especially ordered from Delhi, dry fruits, cakes and *basrakh*. These trays eventually would find their way to the groom's place to be distributed amongst his relatives.

Fatimaji was in a heated conversation with her husband. 'What do you mean we shouldn't keep any money on top of the trays? Didn't we agree that we would keep four five hundred notes on each tray?' she was shouting angrily.

'What can I say?' the poor Latifsaab was mumbling while reaching at his beige-coloured Khan suit pocket.

'Fatimai, did you hear?' said Maqsooda as she walked swiftly towards the harried couple. 'Listen to what your *manzimuour* is saying. There will now be 150 girls from the groom's side for the *mehendi*.'

Fatimaji held her head and would surely have collapsed if her frail husband hadn't been so good at his reflexes. He helped her sit on the carpeted floor while giving Jabbar an enquiring look.

'*Ye kus tawan*! This is a disaster! This can happen only with the girl's family!' she lamented.

'Where will they sit?' Latifsaab shook his bald head from side to side and whispered in a feeble voice.

'Where will they sit? Is that what is bothering you? They will be here any minute and how will we make arrangements for pastries, *wazwaan* and *rotis* at such short notice?'

'Jabbar,' Fatimaji's voice was now icy, 'I knew it. I knew something will happen that will ruin the function.' Clearly, she was coming apart, heaving at her chest and slapping her forehead.

'Fatimai, I'll see what can be done,' Maqsooda stepped in. 'Leave it to me. I have phone numbers of a nearby bakery. In fact, I'll get in touch with a couple of other bakeries for the pastries and *rotis*. I'll talk to the *waza*. Maybe, the dinner guests can go without a few dishes of *wazwaan*. You just continue with your preparation. Also, go and change into that lovely yellow suit you have specially made for the *mehendiraat*.'

Fatimaji gave her a look of relief, but she still had her forehead in furrows. Maqsooda got hold of Jabbar's hand and gestured to him to follow her. They hurriedly left the room where the visibly distraught couple were still wringing their hands and mumbling among themselves.

Jabbar was impressed at how quickly Maqsooda got down to business. She instructed him to go to the small room on the top floor next to the hall where the function was going to start and ask about the number of pastry and cake plates they had set aside. Meanwhile, she would check with the *waza*. She forwarded her mobile number to him and asked him to get in touch without wasting any time after he had got the information. She was already running towards the backyard where the head *waza* Saifuddin and his team of chefs had made elaborate arrangements for the *wazwaan* to be cooked for the function.

As he ran up two steps at a time towards the second floor, Jabbar felt a wave of relief sprinkled with a pinch of happiness spread over him. "*It's going to be alright after all*," he kept reminding himself. The tiny room was flooded with plates laden with pastries, slices of cakes, *katlam* and *kulchas*. There were bowls with dry fruits and toffees, and crates containing tetra packs of *Rani* juice. Three ladies, who had been toiling over making these arrangements, seemed all set to leave when Jabbar reached there.

'You need to give me the number of pastries and cakes you need. You see, the number of plates to be arranged now is 150.'

One of the ladies, who was on the verge of leaving, froze as he spoke. 'But we have to get ready too,' she said angrily, holding her painful back. 'Here,' she gave him a lock and key, 'Go check for yourself. We have to go now.'

Her other two friends had taken flight already, running down the stairs as fast as they could. Jabbar was nonplussed for a moment but had to give in; he had no choice. He entered the windowless suffocating room and was hit by a strong pungent smell. A tiny table fan was whirring in the corner.

He called Maqsooda as he rushed out of the room. 'At least 80 more plates are needed. Let's have some extra. You never know about those idiot relatives of the groom. Who knows how many will hop into the cars at the last moment?'

There she was, sitting next to the head *waza*, even before he could finish the sentence. Saifuddin was all smiles, handing over a succulent roasted lamb kidney to Maqsooda. He was in his 'work' clothes, a *pheran* the colour of ash, which had known better days. Later in the evening, he would change into a spotless white *pheran* while serving the delicacies, the recipes which his family had guarded for generations.

'You must thank your stars, Jigra, that Maqsoodaji took over this crisis. Otherwise, knowing Fatimaji, this would have been the end of your career! She has already informed that nervous fatso and all arrangements are in place. So, you just relax,' Saifuddin said with a twinkle in those ancient eyes.

Calm as a cucumber, Maqsooda was catching up on the latest gossip, not at all bothered by the heat of dozens of *chulas* around her and the noisy *wazas* at work. 'Here, sit down and take a breather,' said Maqsooda. 'What do you prefer, liver or kidneys? Personally, I love a nice kidney with the sprinkling of *sonth* and red chillies.'

Jabbar happily joined in. Soon, he was talking freely, laughing loudly as she mimicked some relatives of the bride. He didn't realise it then, but this was actually the first time that he had spent an enjoyable time with someone other than his transgender family, without getting that dreadful feeling of judgement or ridicule.

'You better be on your way Jigra,' said Saifuddin, 'the guests are about to arrive.'

As the *manzimuour*, he was expected to oversee everything during the function, from the seating arrangements of the guests (the elders and the important relatives of the groom must sit next to the bride) to introducing the groom's and bride's relatives, for he was actually the only person to know who was who.

The hall had all but filled up by the time Jabbar arrived. The guests were not yet there, and already, most of the seats were taken. Small children were running around, some pulling at the curtains. Clapping and shouting loudly, Jabbar managed to get some of them to leave the room. It was to be a long, busy night. Luckily, there were no more hysterics or goof-ups. The womenfolk, who had been reluctant to even vacate their seats just moments back, behaved beautifully as the guests arrived, gathering in one corner of the room to sing the *wanwun*, Kashmiri songs that were fun and teasing, and at the same time full of sadness and pathos. The kids did not jump over each other's heads to get to the toffees and dry fruit that were showered over the guests. And although most of the pastries and cake pieces were returned untouched, at least they did not have a shortage of food.

'How did you manage so many *kebabs* at such short notice?' whispered Jabbar in Maqsooda's ear.

Brushing him off while gently touching her enormous gold *jumkas*, she gave him a coy smile and joined the *wanwun* of the ladies. She had the strongest, most melodious of the voices, and soon, the other ladies were following her lead in a chorus.

Jabbar entered his home just as the morning *azaan* could be heard from the masjid at the corner of the narrow lane which had rows of small modest-looking houses. Exhausted, he hit the bed without even removing his shoes.

'Jigra, it's nearly noon,' called Ayub Bab from the tiny kitchen, where he sat on the floor making *nun chai* on a kerosene stove.

Ayub Bab was in his early fifties, but looked at least eighty. Deep furrows of worry lined his handsome features. His sense of calm seemed to be rattled this morning. When he handed the tea to Jabbar, his back was a little more bent than usual and his breathing heavy. Jabbar looked at him with concern.

'*Kya daleel*. What's the matter?' he enquired.

In return, he just got a weak smile. 'Have your tea. Shall I get you a roti to have with it?'

'No, Baba, but sit here,' said Jabbar. 'You know how I got saved yesterday? You know how Fatimaji is; she would have made sure that I would have to say goodbye to this profession forever! This *maharaza* family was sure to get me doomed,' he went on breathlessly.

'Yes, Yes, I know,' Bab was saying. 'Now get ready, today is a big day. The wedding festivities have just started, you have to make sure nothing goes wrong again.'

'How do you know? When were you there?'

'The head *waza* called me and told me the whole thing. He is known to me, you know.'

'Hmm, but still, why would he want to call you on such a small matter?' asked Jabbar.

'I had asked him to keep an eye on you and help you since this job was so important to you,' replied Bab. 'You better be there before the *nikah* guests arrive.'

After Jabbar left, Ayub Bab sat down near the narrow window that looked out at a dirty street where a few strays roamed around looking for food. He was in deep thought. Jabbar had been with him since the day he was born. He could never forget that chilly winter morning nearly 25 years ago. He had been waiting outside a *harissa* shop, hunched on his feet, taking long puffs from a *jajeer* that was being passed on between a dozen men, mostly domestic helps, waiting for their turn to collect the special breakfast delicacy for their household. Mushtaq was there too. Ayub had never met him before, but as the elderly man started chatting with his friends, he kept eye contact with Ayub. It seemed that the information he was sharing with his friends was actually directed towards Ayub.

As he gathered a little closer, he heard him whisper, 'The baby's genitals are not fully formed. A male, but incomplete.'

'A *lanche*!' his audience gasped. 'What will they do with the baby?'

'You know how it is with these *lanche* fellows. They will take him away! Or the parents will murder him'

Ayub held his *kangri* closer to his chest and mustered the courage to ask Mushtaq, 'Where? Where is the baby?'

Mushtaq's kind eyes lit up. Patting him gently, he said, 'Anyone who could bring up this child as his own would not be any less than a *farishta*, an angel. His father will not let him live and his mother will not be able to keep him.'

Ayub had immediately left for the hospital Mushtaq had mentioned. It was easy to locate the father of the baby. Standing outside the recovery room, he was surrounded by womenfolk of his family.

'*Ye gayi lanat*! Your wife has brought shame to the family!' they harried him with their taunts.

'What are you planning now?' said a heavyset woman in a colourful *pheran* and matching headscarf.

Her daughter, who seemingly couldn't get over the scandal, had her hand over her mouth 'We can't get *it* home, *baijana*. My in-laws will throw me out if they find out.'

Ayub had slowly approached the group. 'Your servant Mushtaq said you had some work for me,' he had said haltingly.

The man looked up and seeing the sense of relief on his face, his mother and sister beamed together.

'Here, Allah has sent his messenger,' the mother said. The three crowded around Ayub. 'Sit, sit,' she said, pinning him on a plastic chair with her large fleshy hands. 'Look. My daughter-in-law has just delivered a baby. It's like you. I mean, it's neither a boy nor a girl. We cannot take *it* home. My husband will kill both the baby and the mother.' After taking a deep breath, she continued, 'Will you take *it* with you? We will give you some money too. We only want to save the baby; nothing else.' How her eyes had lied. It was plain in sight that they only cared for their reputation.

Ayub, who until that moment was not sure what he intended to do, immediately knew that he had to save the baby. Suddenly, he felt his shoulders sag as if a huge boulder was placed on them. The white shirt he was wearing under his *pheran* was damp with sweat even in this winter chill, and his heart had started to beat faster. "*They got rid of the baby, in the same way, they must be rushing out to hand over the garbage to the garbage collector, impatient and not once looking back*", he thought.

All his life, Ayub had been lonely and miserable. He was born in a world which had very little room for people like him. He had never known his biological parents, and never ever got a straight answer from Najam whenever curiosity got the better of him. Najam, forever singing to him, telling him stories of faraway lands, monsters and palaces, ants and butterflies, fish and snakes and *jinns*, had a different version of how he had adopted Ayub, depending mostly on his mood. In the afternoons, when the rest of the household where Najam worked as a domestic help was resting, he would often snatch a few moments of leisure. Getting hold of his two favourite companions, his *jajeer* and *kangri*, he would sit on the veranda overlooking the large garden of his master's house.

'It was a warm, sunny day. One of my friends had a taxi. So, the four of us went to Nishat Bagh. We packed some *wazwaan*, a stove and a *jajeer* and had a great time there. The flowers were the loveliest that year. We could smell them from the Boulevard! I had gone to wash my hands in the fountain and saw a white bundle lying behind a giant chinar. It was moving. I don't know why I moved towards it; it could have been anything: a bomb, an animal, it could be dangerous!' he would say excitedly. 'But then, it was just you, a tiny baby wrapped in a dirty towel, without even a diaper!'

His other version was not so interesting though. A Maulvi Sahab he knew, had simply handed him over the new born, saying he had found him crying at the steps of the Maqhdoom Saahib shrine. To Ayub's mind, this story seemed more plausible. Ayub too never got around to telling Jabbar about the real story of his past. The youngster had so many of his own battles to face; his heart would have broken had he known the cruelty of his own parents towards him.

Ayub had single-handedly brought him up, protecting him from every jibe, every insult hurled his way. Jabbar had believed Ayub when he told him that a *pari*, a fairy, had flown all the way from *jannat* and had left him at his bedside. He had supposedly caught a glimpse of her as she flew back to the heavens. She wore a long shimmering dress, had golden hair and silver wings, was his description of the fairy. In the later years, he simply denied that he had seen her. Instead, he said he had been woken up by the cries of the baby next to his bed. But the scent in the room, he said, had been so divine that he knew that an extraordinary event had happened in his bedroom that night and he had been visited by one of Allah's apostles. Jabbar had found great comfort in these words.

Jabbar soon realised that coming out of Ayub Bab's cosy embrace and walking into the real world wasn't easy at all. He heard the word '*lanchekot*' hurled at him as he was leaving a grocery shop one evening. His reflexes got the better of him and he doubly retraced his steps to confront the two boys who were standing there with their arms crossed, challenging him. But the shopkeeper hurriedly appeared between them, and while angrily pointing at the door, asked Jabbar to leave. '*Nasa*, not in my shop. I don't want any trouble here.'

Jabbar had to leave, red-faced and in shame, while two pairs of eyes burnt his back. He had not eaten or slept that night. On Ayub Bab's prodding, he told him about the incident. Grabbing a *jajeer*, he took a long drag and wept hot tears of frustration. Ayub Bab got him a glass of water and sat with him throughout the night. They did not talk; they just shared the *jajeer* and looked out of the window at the half-crest moon.

'*Hya, che kyoho goy,* what's the matter?' Sanam had asked the next morning, patting his back. 'You look like a *murda*, a dead body,' he had jokingly said. 'Look, these things do not matter. Whatever they say, how does it matter?' Pointing at Ayub, he said, 'All that matters is love,' and then, mimicking Dev Anand he made an exaggerated bow, and in the legend's accent, added, 'And friendship. You have both. You are very blessed, *meri jaan*. Most people would die for that.'

It was late that night when the jackals could be heard howling away, Sanam and Jabbar stole away to sit under the lone chinar, which was in an isolated field, their favourite place since they were kids. Sanam was younger to Jabbar by a year, and like him, had faced a lot of taunts from childhood about his gender.

'*Naba, yeh gov galat*! How wrong you are! You should be proud of your gender, not think like them. You will face this ridicule for the rest of your life, so what are you going to do? Commit suicide. Allah has made us like this. I'm not bothered about anyone saying anything, and you shouldn't too. We are not inferior; we are special,' said Sanam, making a heart shape with his two hands.

This folding of the two hands into a heart shape would later become their own private code to lift each other's spirits; to say I'm here, we are in this together.

The wedding venue was chaotic. The elderly family members had notched up their forehead furrows and the youngsters were moving around the tents looking like they were busy with some urgent errands. Jabbar had gained some confidence after yesterday's near disaster. The *nikah* guests from the groom's family and the *moulvi* sahib were having *kehwa*, and the bride's family was congratulating her. Tears were running down the cheeks of her mother. Fatimaji's mother-in-law was patting her shoulder.

The old woman, while holding the door knob for support, was telling her in her feeble voice, 'Daughters are born to be given away. It is their *taqdeer*, their destiny.'

"*My mother-in-law never had a daughter of her own and so, would never know the pain of giving away a piece of heart to an unknown person,*" thought Fatimaji bitterly. Jabbar did not have a minute to rest. He felt like he was on a rollercoaster ride. As the time for *ruksati* got near, Fatimaji was getting more and more flustered. She was bitterly sobbing and wailing as her darling daughter walked towards the car with her handsome groom in tow.

Jabbar's job was not yet done. The *walima* was the next day. This was one chance for one-upmanship for the groom's family. The guest list would be of at least 1000 people. Every member of the bride's family would be there with their extended families too. They would be fed a lavish 20-course *wazwaan* and four enormous tents in the groom's and the adjoining lawns of the neighbour's had been erected for the occasion. Gone were the days when lunch would be wrapped up by 4 P.M. These days, by the time the men finished eating, it was evening time, and on some occasions, lunch was served at 6 P.M. to the poor famished ladies. Jabbar was tired to the bone and was just leaving for home when he saw Latifsaab approaching him.

'Jabbara, Jigra,' he said affectionately. 'Here, keep this cash,' he said, handing out a newspaper-wrapped bundle to him.

As Jabbar opened it, he felt hurt and angry at the same time. It was just half of what was promised to him.

He began to protest, but Latifsaab just patted his back and with a half-smile, he said, 'Don't worry. I never keep *karz*. I will pay you. Meanwhile, keep this. By the way, I've heard the groom's mother is going to give you a gold coin. You really deserve it.'

He left before Jabbar could plead with him some more. Saifuddin, the head *waza*, who had overheard the conversation approached him and held his hand.

Taking him outside he asked, 'So, he paid you less too?'

'Half, can you imagine!' replied Jabbar angrily.

'*Kath bozu*, Listen, leave all this. I need to talk to you.' Taking his *jajeer* with him, Saifuddin settled down on an old rug.

'Can we talk tomorrow? I'm tired,' said Jabbar.

'You can sleep here. We have an empty bed.'

'No, *shukriya*.' Jabbar got up to leave.

'It's about your mother.'

Startled, Jabbar sat down with a thud. For a moment, he lost his bearing. As he looked into Saifuddin's kind eyes, he knew that he was not joking.

'My mother,' Jabbar said slowly, his heartbeat quickening.

'Yes, she's here. At this wedding. And you have met her.'

'Who?' Jabbar asked in a choked voice.

Even before Saifuddin had spelt out his mother's name, the pleasant face of Maqsooda flashed in his mind. 'She was here with you yesterday at this very place you are sitting.'

Jabbar could feel his whole body relax, but his heart was beating fast. His hand flew to his chest, as if he had been shot. His mind was in turmoil. Was this an utter sense of ecstasy or was his heart breaking into a million pieces? His eyes were watery and his hands trembling.

'*Moaj*. Mother,' he kept whispering to himself.

Saifuddin was watching him closely. 'Your Bab did not want to tell you yet. But I don't want you to have that vacuum of not knowing your mother. It's like a hole inside the body; it can never be filled. Knowing her will heal you and give you *himmat*, strength. You will not suffer like your poor Bab, who seems to be losing himself and his bearings. Did you notice he looks like a *lachulitul*, a broomstick?' Saifuddin came closer to Jabbar. While wiping his tears, he said, 'Jigara, knowing your birth mother is enough for you. I just wanted you to know. You don't have to stand at her door and ask her to take you in.'

'Does she know?' Jabbar whispered, with a glimmer in his eyes.

'No,' Saifuddin sighed. 'And I don't think she should be told. *Khabar cha*, Allah only knows what the poor woman has been through.'

A sudden rage took over Jabbar. 'What she has gone through? *Ahanu be osus na haiwan zaamut!* She gave birth to a monster, of course, she must be ashamed of me. So, what did she do? Did she throw me in a dustbin? Is that where Bab found me?'

'No, No, Jigara. *Kyoho goy.* Don't say all that. It's not what happened.' Saifuddin then went on to narrate the happenings of that fateful night when his friend Ayub came to him with a new born baby.

'You had always said the life of a transgender is like that of an ant. No trace left of its existence and no one to mourn its death. Well, today, I prove you wrong. I have given birth and he will not let my name fade away. I will give him so much love that he will mourn my passing as he would for his own parents,' he had said.

'Your mother was still in the operation theatre when your father handed you over to Ayub. She was told that the baby died.' A sad tone came over his voice. 'But they never stopped tormenting her about your gender.'

'How do you know all this?' Jabbar asked, surprised.

'I have known the family for a long time now. My family has been cooking their *wazwaan* for generations. I keep a tab on my clients. In fact, I was there at their house the night you were born. It was your uncle's *mehendiraat*. Your mother was taken to the hospital that night. The next morning, we heard that the baby had died. When Ayub came with a baby to me, I put two and two together.'

Both were in deep thought for a long time. What a strange world! Mother and son are forced to live separate lives, deprived of each other's love. '*It's like cutting a person into pieces and throwing the pieces to jackals,*' thought Saifuddin. Jabbar's body was limp and exhausted, but his eyes had lit up and a peaceful calmness had descended on him. He was looking around in wonder, as if he had just been born, and was seeing the world for the first time. Tingling sensations, fresh smells and bright sights were making him dizzy. He got up to hug Saifuddin.

'Go home now. Go to Ayub. He must be waiting for you,' Saifuddin said.

One look at Jabbar's face, and Ayub knew that something had changed. No words were exchanged between them; their tears and hugs did all the talking. Jabbar fell asleep as Ayub cradled his head, rocking him gently just as he would when he was little. He found himself in the same position when he woke the next morning.

'Bab, did you not sleep?' he asked.

'How could I? I was watching my beautiful child. Remember, I am always here for you. Nothing will ever change that.'

'And I for you, Baba,' replied Jabbar, bringing fresh tears to Ayub's eyes.

Chapter 2
Maqsooda

The birth of the girl was an occasion of great joy to the family. After all, she was the only girl in the *khandaan*. Maqsooda had been treated no less than a princess, pampered and loved by her numerous *chachus, chachis, maasis* and their families. And she showered each of them with affection and care in return. She would carefully jot down every birthday and anniversary in her pink diary ever since she learnt to read and write. She made sure to telephone them and send cards, flowers and gifts on every occasion. She was pious and God-fearing. And she also was the heart and soul of her household, which consisted of her three brothers and parents.

Her marriage to Dr. Fayaz was celebrated with great pomp and show, as every detail, her dowry – the gifts to the groom's family – the menu and the grand decorations in the sprawling lawns of their ancestral house had been immaculately looked into by her doting parents. But the birth of a girl saw the first fissure in her marriage. She knew she had finally hit rock bottom when her husband entered her hospital room after her second delivery and announced to Maqsooda, whose brain was still foggy due to the anaesthesia, that she was no more welcome in his house. She shivered as she tried to make sense of what he was saying. Perhaps she was delirious.

She attempted a weak smile and asked, 'Where is my baby? Is it a boy?'

Hearing this, Dr. Fayaz shouted. '*Che aosuy dohoy shikas*. You have brought nothing but ruin to our lives. And this takes the cake! Yes, you had a child, a *lanche*,' he said with a bitter laugh.

'But where is he?' she asked softly.

Just then his mother and sister entered the room.

'She wants to know where the *lanche* is,' he was laughing loudly now.

Shaking her hands in front of the daughter-in-law, in a way of a curse, the mother-in-law said, 'Your bastard baby is dead. Thank Allah for that. And you are dead to us, you shameless bitch.' She spat on the ground and said, 'Don't ever try to come back to our house.'

In a weak voice, she asked her husband if she could take Seher, her two-year-old, with her. She shuddered and clutched her heart when he hurled abuses at her.

'Get out of our lives. She is not your daughter. And if you ever try to claim her, I will see that you suffer. Be grateful that I'm just sending you to your father's house and not shooting you on your face.'

They had left her there. Just like that.

Like a broken doll, she kept sitting in a corner of her room for days. Each of her family members took turns convincing her to go back to her husband, she had a daughter to look after. Sometimes, the thought of Seher did bring back a spark in her. She argued with herself. *'They cannot do this! I have every right to her custody. She's just two!'* But then Dr. Fayaz's fierce gaze and icy voice took over and she collapsed into a heap once again.

A year passed. By now, she was a pale shadow of herself. Seher had started school. Her mother would stand outside the school gate for hours, behind a large tree that hid her completely, just to get a glimpse of her. She nearly went out of her mind when while returning home, two policemen stopped her and told her she had been banned from contacting her daughter. She had shouted and screamed.

But they were very calm. 'Madam, your divorce papers have reached your parents. It is very clear that you are not allowed to visit your daughter from now on. This is the only condition of Doctorsahib. *Su chu na khodgaraz, nat nach nawihi*, He has been most generous. Otherwise, he could make you bite the dust.'

That night was the longest in her life. She had a long conversation with herself. Every aspect of her life was brought to focus, dissected and analysed. The glow of love in her heart for her parents did not grow smaller. Although it took a while to understand, she knew they did not have a choice but to send her back to her husband. A lot of their standing in society depended on the success of the marriage of their only daughter. Yet, a nagging thought sent electric currents through her body. What society? Is it bigger than their daughter's future, her life? The agony of a loveless marriage writhed like a serpent in her chest. A man who could not stand up to his wife, who refused to accept the fact that he was father to a girl, and later, separated her from her mother, knowing well that she was the only lifeline of his traumatized wife. The pain of losing two children brought a downpour of tears. The taunts of her husband and his family rang in her ears, and she doubled up while holding herself tight, rolling on the bed as if her body was on fire.

Maqsooda had died and was reborn that night. The words in her diary wept softly too.

My hands hurt. I have been digging my own grave throughout the night. Let this night end swiftly, my Maula, so that I can crawl into my grave and sleep!

She pulled her hair and beat her chest. She wailed loudly. And when she was spent, she just kept looking at the darkness. Her mother saw her the next morning looking like a corpse, completely still, her skin white and her eyes vacant.

'*Moj lagi balai,*' she said, taking her into her arms. '*Wain kya suchut?*' What have you decided?

'He wants a divorce, Moji.'

Her mother's lips were a thin line now. She gave Maqsooda a push and left the room with the chilling words, '*Che asak hamesha ase kyich laanat.* You have always brought us the worst tidings.'

No one disturbed her after that day. A deafening silence descended on the household. For Maqsooda, time lost its dimensions. A dense fog had settled in her brain as if she was drugged. It took immense strength to give herself a long, hard look in the mirror. A look of horror came over her. A complete stranger, haggard and hollow to the bone, stared back at her. There was a radical shift in her thought process at that moment. No one is responsible, hence there's no one to blame. She owed it only to herself and herself alone. She owed it to herself to pick up the thread of her life and move ahead. All her life she had lived in the shadow of her parents who had told her what to do and how to behave. She thought that was happiness, thanking the Almighty at every step of the way. But it took them just a moment to pull away their supportive hands. And now, she owed it to herself to make her own path.

Maqsooda stood at the kitchen door, her eyes downcast, waiting for her father to speak, or say anything to her. But he just sat on the low *chowki* quietly, his head resting against a wall, eyes closed.

She mustered the courage to call him. 'Baba,' she said softly. '*Ijazat diyiv*, give me permission to leave.'

She, his princess, his heart and soul, was leaving. Yet, he sat there motionless, emotionless. Years later, when she thought about this scene, she was actually grateful that there had been no drama involved when she left home that day, never to come back. It would have made her weak in her resolve to start life afresh, to make a clean break from the past.

From now on, she would keep her step light, look at her life and the people around her with new eyes, and above all, would be her own best friend. One day at a time, one step at a time became the motto that helped her manoeuvre through a long dark tunnel. Her faith imbibed her being with a sense of calm. This new found strength gave her enough energy to let happiness seep in, drop by drop. Like a butterfly that has just emerged from its cocoon, she too looked at her wings with amazement and delight. There was no space for regrets, bitterness or anger.

Her path was crisscrossed with new relationships – friends and colleagues. Her youth and beauty attracted marriage proposals too, but she would never walk that path again. She had just started taking baby-steps towards life. There was the whole world to explore!

Maqsooda had watched her daughter, Seher, from afar, grow from a shy little plump girl to a lovely young woman. She had spied on her Facebook page just to have a look at her beautiful smile. She was proud of her achievements. Her daughter was a brilliant doctor and had the courage to choose her own life partner.

As she drove back home from Naazu's wedding, for some unknown reason, her thoughts flew to her still born child. A wave of sadness passed over her as she remembered that she had never got a chance to hold him even once or to say goodbye. She silently sent a prayer for him to the heavens.

THE END

DRIFTWOOD

Chapter 1

The dark filthy water was moving in a circular motion. Slowly at first, but soon, gaining speed. It looked like it was being churned by a giant hand mixer. It made me dizzy. I seemed to be rooted at the bank of this putrid pond. I couldn't move a muscle. Maybe, I was paralyzed. The breeze was cold and a slow hum could be distinctly heard coming from the bottom of the dark deep pond. However, it was mostly the smell that made me sick. The smell of rotten flesh drove a wave of nausea through my very core. A sudden jolt and I was running. A dull thud and total darkness.

I was lucky, because minutes later, I had been found sprawled on the tiles of my bathroom by Mogal Ded, the house help. As I looked around, my confused brain tried to make sense of the half-dozen eyes directly above my head. Their loud voices were giving me a headache. Gasping for breath, I tried to move away from Mummy, Abu and Mogal Ded who had crowded next to me, suffocating me.

After what seemed ages, Abu said with a sense of irritation, 'Move away. Let her breathe some fresh air.'

Holding my head, I blinked hard.

'What happened, Jaan?' Mummy said, her voice laced with concern.

'I don't know! Why do you shout so loudly when you have to call me for dinner? I must have dozed off while studying. The next thing I remember is you shouting at the top of your voice! I just ran towards the bathroom to wash my hands and here I am!'

Dad had a theory that seemed sensible enough. 'The brain was still asleep and your body went against its commands! *Yeh to hona hi tha, shukr* there was no major damage,' he tried to placate me while glaring at Mummy. 'Hafiza, next time you want to call her, knock on her door gently, ask for permission to enter and politely ask her when she would like to have dinner.'

Mummy looked at him, rolled her eyes and said, '*Ji Huzoor*.' Bowing her head, she left the room in a huff, with Mogal Ded hurriedly following her.

'Sabi, please be careful next time. You could have hurt yourself. Now, come downstairs for dinner.' Abu gave me a hug and kissed my forehead.

I had completely forgotten about the dream. That night, as I stared at the pages of my lesson on drainage systems of ancient India, I suddenly got an uncomfortable feeling in the pit of my stomach. The black and white blurry pictures of wells and drains started swimming in front of my eyes. And the text! I had to squint my eyes to see it clearly. It certainly did not look like English to me. I closed my eyes and sat back, resting my head on the red and white giant bolster. "*It must be the fall! Maybe I've had a concussion,*" I thought. It was time to hit the sack. There was enough time to prepare for the SST exam thankfully. As I reached for the book, the words still looked alien to me. "*This certainly is not English,*" I wondered. The world was suddenly spinning fast around me, and I lost consciousness before I could call for help.

Abu kept giving me anxious looks the next morning during breakfast. As was his habit, he was hunched over his plate, with his face nearly touching the *dastarkhwan*. His right leg twitched involuntarily, an indication of his nervousness.

He had a barrage of questions for me. 'Did you sleep well, Beta? Does your head hurt?'

I took a sip of *nun chai* and asked Mogal Ded, who was hovering nearby, to get me some more *malai*.

Mummy was buttering the *rotis* brought from the neighbourhood *kandur* and muttering angrily 'Mogli, why do you always get cold and soft *rotis*? Every time I go to Nuzhat's place, I realize the boy, Tariq, has brought crisp, hot ones for them. Stop loitering around the *kandurwaan*, and come back home as soon as you get the *rotis*.'

I was staring at my *nun chai* cup which was brimming with cream. 'Mummy, what is this?' I said pushing it away. 'I want something sweeter.'

Mummy looked at me in surprise. 'Really, all these years I have been telling you not to have *nun chai* first thing in the morning. It will give you ulcers; I've always been saying. And you never listened. Ever since you turned 10 you demanded *nun chai* every day and haven't changed it for the last 6 years. And here you are! You hate *nun chai!* Good for you. Mogli will make a *Lipton chai* for you.'

It was a strange feeling, this repulsion, this intense craving for something sweet and…eggs. Yes, I wanted an omelette too.

'Mogal Ded, can you make me an omelette too, but plain, only salt and pepper.'

Mummy gave me an encouraging smile, and Abu's leg was no more twitching.

'And a coffee. Black,' I said.

'No. No. You will ruin your stomach. No black coffee in the morning,' Mummy said angrily.

'Ok, I don't want anything then,' I said, shrugging and wiping the tears that were ready to drop.

'It's ok, Jaanu, have your coffee,' Daddy patted my back.

'*Kya sa chuk karan. Andram gas nas kharab,*' protested Mummy. She was concerned about my acidic stomach like every Kashmiri mother. Dad just gave her a stern look and she didn't say a word after that.

'Can I have jam on my toast too, please?' I said.

My room felt icy when I entered it. I checked if a window was open. To my surprise, none was. I switched on the heater and looked for the *pheran* that was lying on the bottom shelf of my wardrobe – one that Mummy had forced me to keep, one that I never intended to wear. But today was too chilly, I thought. In fact, I'll need a scarf too. I huddled up in the thick tiger design blanket that had been my favourite for years. It was a gift by Danish Mamu who had brought it all the way from Dubai.

Mentally, I was calculating the number of hours left for the SST exam, the number of chapters I had still not touched and the hours required for revision. It helped to stay organized and focused during final exams, especially since I had not really paid much attention to my books the rest of the year. As I stared at the SST book, a chill went down my spine. This was not my book. It had mysteriously been switched. It was written in a strange language! I hurriedly went through my bag and scattered all the books on my bed. All of them had been switched! What is this joke?

I rushed out of the room and ran downstairs.

Abu immediately chided me for running so fast down the stairs. 'Didn't you learn your lesson yesterday? Do you want to have another fainting spell?' he said angrily.

I just got hold of his arm and pulled him out of the room. 'Please come with me, Abujaan. I want to show you something.'

He must have sensed the urgency in my voice because he followed me to my room without another word.

'There, look at my books. Someone switched them. I have an exam tomorrow and I don't have my books!' I was hysterical by now.

He looked at the books, puzzled and bewildered. 'How can this be? Who can do this?' He searched my notebooks and as he saw their contents, his hands flew to his head. 'Why do you write in a coded language? Where did you learn that?' He was looking at me directly now. 'Sabi, what is this?'

'I don't know, Abu.'

'I think you know, Sabi. Did you do this deliberately to avoid taking exams?'

'No, Abujaan'

'*Kya Daleel*? I don't understand, Sabi. Why don't you want to take exams? Don't you want to go to the next class? It's a crucial year. Next year is your class 12 and after that, medical college. You are spoiling your career!'

'I'm already a doctor. A famous one too. I don't need to go to college again!'

Abu was looking at me strangely. He took a step back.

'What's the matter? Sabi, stop it at once!'

'Stop what?'

'Stop playing games. Get down to your studies. There's hardly any time left for your exam'

As I paced around the room blowing imaginary rings in the air, he came after me and grabbed my hand.

'Have you been taking drugs? What are you taking?' he said as his grip became tighter around my wrist.

The next moment I saw him flying across the room. A big thud could be heard as his back hit the wooden door. I continued pacing the room, smoking my imaginary cigarette without giving him another glance.

"*This room is too stuffy,*" I thought, pacing at a furtive pace. I need a bigger mattress too. I was throwing things – pillows, books, stuffed toys – everything that got in my way, out of the window. I needed to breathe; I needed a bigger space. My space. Just then, the three figures appeared at the door. They had nothing to say, except stare with their eyes popped. I slammed the door on their faces.

Chapter 2

~~~~

I cannot see my reflection in the water; it's that murky. And it stinks. Something floating over it, almost hidden by the bushes, catches my attention. The bright moonlight casts a shimmer over the figure of a person, most probably dead. As I hurry towards it, my heart beats faster as if I know who it is. It's me in my white *salwar-kameez* school uniform. I know, because I'm wearing my Newton House yellow sash and the prefect's badge. So, this is what it feels like when you are dead! Nothing! Just cold, so cold, a shiver went down my spine. And it's dark and bleak out here. Maybe, I still have a distance to cover to reach heaven, or is it hell? Or maybe, it's just a dream.

It wasn't a dream after all! Because, here I was, back in the room. Everything was the same except me; I wasn't there. I was still floating over that murky water, somewhere between earth and heaven or hell! There was a stocky man in my room. He had strapped a machine on my arm and was measuring my BP. Another man in a check housecoat stood nearby. Two women peered from behind his shoulder.

'It's normal,' he declared finally, 'BP normal.'

'But Doctorsaahib, she's behaving very strangely. *Khabar kya gos? Fever maa chus?*'

'She?' I growled, 'Did you call me "She?"' The man looked up in surprise. 'Sabi, *Jigra, Gobra*, come here. Tell me, *beta*, what's the matter? You were studying for your exam, got up suddenly and had a fall. This was the day before yesterday. You have been acting strange ever since. You somehow, I don't know how and why changed your books to a foreign language and yesterday, you hit me,' he said with indignation, 'hit your father!'

'Why do you call me, Sabi? I'm Trevor.' Hearing this, shocked the two women. They shrieked loudly. The man just stood there, hitting his head in exasperation.

The doctor seemed amused though! 'Where did she pick that American accent?'

'I'm French, not American,' I corrected him.

'Sabi, enough of this nonsense,' said the man in the check housecoat loudly in an angry tone. 'You have missed today's exam. If this is what you wanted to achieve, you have had your way! You are trying to harm your own career, your own life.'

'I'm a doctor,' I said, 'I don't need any other career. I love my job!'

One of the women, the fat one, who was getting more and more anxious every moment, stepped forward and tried to hug me. I pushed her away. Her shoulder cracked at my touch and she started screaming loudly. Holding her tightly, the other woman said, '*Amis has chuy jinn chamut*, a *jinn* has entered Sabi's body.'

The doctor said to the man in the check housecoat, 'We have to take her to the hospital immediately. I think it's a major fracture.'

'You can bet. Her scapula is beyond repair,' I said, laughing now.

Chapter 3

~~~~

I was starving. Where do they keep the food? The kitchen was most likely downstairs. The door was locked from the outside. What a stupid thing to do. With one blow, the door broke into two. There was no one downstairs. Finding the fridge was easy. No bread. A lot of butter and half a dozen bowls with some spicy dishes. Wait, are these meatballs? I hunted for a knife and fork, but the spoon stand had only spoons. Will have to do with a spoon then.

There was more pandemonium. I was wolfing down the meatballs and gulping coke in the kitchen when I heard a noise. The scrawny lady stood in front of me brandishing a large dirty broom in front of my face.

'Enough, get out of here,' I growled.

'*Be chas ne kochan*. I don't fear you. Now, get the hell out of her body. *Allah ka wasta*,' she shouted hysterically. '*Allah ka wasta*,' she said repeatedly.

I wanted to smash her face, but I didn't. I simply left her gaping at me, and muttering away, ran upstairs.

There were more people in the room that day. Strangers came and stared at me from a distance. They whispered to each other and were gone. Late in the evening, the strangest of them all entered the room and came close to the bed I was resting on. He seemed shapeless to me. No matter how much I tried, I couldn't make eye contact with him. He stood in front of me for a long time. Just observing me. I wanted him to leave, I wanted to shout at him, and I wanted to throw him out of the window, but I didn't do any of that. I just curled myself into a ball and turned away from his piercing eyes.

But I was just pretending, of course. I knew he had been brought in to kick me out, throw me out of my own house where I had been living long before any of them came to this world. I stood up to my full height.

My booming laughter echoed from the wooden ceiling. 'Are you here to scare me?'

The man who wore a long dark gown, just stood there, making knots in a long red cloth he took out from his pocket. He left as suddenly as he had appeared, but not before gently placing the cloth with the knots on the bed.

That red piece of cloth, sitting so innocently on the bed, fascinated as well as excited me. I knew this was deliberately put there to destroy me. The more I looked at it, the more it looked like it had moved, ever so gently, more like a single flame of fire. I laughed at the thought. It's nothing. I tried to ignore it, but my eyes were drawn to it. I went close to it and touched a triangular corner that was jutting out. A shock ran through my veins. It was as if I had touched a hot amber. I went to the other end of the bed and watched the cloth with interest. It was indeed made of fire!

A giggle that started as a tiny ripple in my belly soon turned into a spasm. I laughed loudly, holding my stomach, I rolled on the bed, shaking all over. He had the gall to make ME fearful! I, who has crossed realms, time and space, who cannot be separated from nature itself, would be scared by a mere piece of cloth! I rushed towards the burning ambers, picked them up with both hands and threw them out of the window.

Chapter 4

I was transported to where my body lay. Entwined by the bushes, near the banks of a dirty pond, there I floated with my face upwards, eyes closed. I could hear a slow hum, which soon took the form of words. 'Go back to where you came from.' 'Go back to your place in this universe.' 'Go back to your own people.' 'Go back to where you belong.' 'Go back to where you will be loved and respected.' 'Go back.' The chanting went on and on in my head.

'But this is my body. This is what I have wanted, after crossing so many dimensions I finally found what I like. How can I let it go? I will not, cannot let it go.'

I tried to wade towards my beloved body, but it looked like I was getting heavier and heavier and couldn't manage even a tiny movement. The water was slowly turning into quicksand.

'Your place is not here. This is not your home. All you will find here is despise and hatred. You cannot rule over people by your strength alone. Soon, they will stop fearing you as well. Go back to your own people. Go back where you are wanted and respected. Go back.'

I stood rooted there for what seemed a lifetime, a million years, staring at my beautiful body. A new feeling went through me like a current. Envy.

Eventually, I was bereft of any strength. I gave up the struggle and just stood still. The darkness, the quiet; I will never forget that. The quicksand slowly seemed to give way to water which had begun to feel more like air, because I was falling, falling into a never-ending abyss.

Haji Saahib ran upstairs when he heard Sabi's screams. 'What has happened to my room?' Where are my things?' She was running from one corner to the other, looking for the favourite things she had so lovingly purchased for her room. She gave a cry of agony as she saw the heap outside her window.

'Abuji, who did this?' she cried.

He took her in his arms and cried tears of relief. '*Shukr Alhamdullilah! Shukr,*' he kept repeating to himself.

THE END

SHADOW

Chapter 1

'We will be landing in New Delhi shortly,' the announcement filled Sanjana with trepidation. She mentally counted to ten and started taking deep breaths. She needed to calm down; there was no way she could lower her carefully crafted mask. Mummy, Papa. Kia... She bit her lip as she thought about her youngest daughter, the one who never left her thoughts, the one she left behind, the one who would never love her back.

Sanjana looked at her mother's frail figure from far away and a lump formed in her throat. Draped in a brown sari and a maroon shawl with auburn chinar leaves embroidered on it, her mother waved as soon as she spotted Sanjana.

Arms drawn out before she could even reach her, she was saying, '*Maej laji balai. Aykha*, You have come to mother!'

Teary-eyed, they hugged tightly.

'Mom, you have become so thin. Are you all right?'

'I am now, *tu aa gayi na. Ab main theek hoon.* Papa is getting the car from the parking.'

The drive to their Defence Colony home was mostly filled with her mother's questions about her family in America.

'*Bittuji cha waray?* How is my dashing son-in-law Bittuji?' She could never call Vineet by his real name.

For her, he would always remain Bittuji – a name he detested, and which he hoped was buried in his past as soon as he left for America, three decades back. Sanjana smiled. Hearing him being called 'Bittuji' gave her a sort of sadistic pleasure.

'*Aur meri potiyan*? Why didn't you get my granddaughters too?'

She did not have the heart to tell her mother that Sonal and Mahi had grown wings. They had long flown out of the nest. She heard snippets about what was going on in their lives whenever she eavesdropped on conversations between her husband and in-laws. Once they were settled in their respective jobs and apartments, they lived away from home as much as possible, rarely communicating with their father and never with their mother.

Sanjana mustered the courage to ask the one question that was bothering her ever since she arrived. 'Kia didn't come to receive me?'

Her father turned to look sharply at her.

'She's not home. She left for Kasol yesterday,' said her mother with a nervous laugh, adding, 'Youngsters these days don't like to be told anything. They have a mind of their own.'

Sanjana let out a loud sigh, which her mother interpreted as disappointment. She touched her daughter's shoulder lightly and said, 'She's your child after all. Give her time. She will come around eventually.'

'She is as obstinate as you,' her father said suddenly.

'Pranji, won't you let the poor girl breathe? She has come from so far away, she must be tired,' his wife retorted. 'Sanju *beta*, don't worry about Kia. She's a very nice kid. And, did Papa tell you how well she plays tennis?'

'Does she? No, Mummy. Papa never tells me anything, especially about Kia,' Sanjana said, with a hint of despair.

She had tears in her eyes, but she wiped them before they could embarrass her in front of her parents. There was no way she would allow that to happen.

'She has been selected for the Nationals, Sanjana. She is a very hardworking girl,' her mother said.

'In that case, she should have been around for practice. Why did you allow her to go to Kasol?'

'*Beta*...' before her mother could complete her sentence, her father said, rather rudely, 'Kia is our responsibility. You don't have to worry or interfere in her life. Just finish the work you have come for, and go back to your family.'

This time, the tears fell freely. She did not even bother to wipe them.

Chapter 2

Jet lagged and exhausted, Sanjana spent a restless night. The past and present were playing like a 36mm movie reel in her head, making her increasingly perplexed with every passing moment. She recollected a time when she was small, she threw a tantrum if Papa didn't give her a tight hug and kiss first thing every morning. A strict disciplinarian, adherence to his rules was something that Professor Pran Nath Dhar managed to reinforce to a marginal degree in the rest of the household, but his demeanour would soften and all defences lower in front of his daughter. There were no rules set for her. He played to her every whim and fancy, sometimes to the utter disapproval of her mother.

Papa made sure that Karan, her brother who was elder to her by three years, would go for his daily runs early every morning, sometimes even when it was snowing in Srinagar. He studied for two hours every evening, and two hours of chess practice before sleep were mandatory for him, no matter what. He could get a respite on only Sundays when he was allowed to play for a while with his friends. As they grew older, Papa continued to shower her with adulation, while strictly micro-monitoring his son's every movement, whether he liked it or not.

Prof. Dhar's temper was well known, not only at home but also at the university where he taught physics. He was nicknamed '*Pranhachkal*' – one whose brain is made of wood, by the merciless students, perhaps, because of his unforgiving nature. It was true that he did not have patience for incompetent, lazy or sloppy behaviour. 'These', he told his students time and again 'were evil forces that could drive a perfectly intelligent student to destroy his future.' He made this very clear from the very first day of meeting them that his life's mission was to guide them to a successful career. He often likened himself to a sherpa who guided climbers to Everest. He knew all the pits and perils of the arduous climb, but only the ones willing to work hard and stay focused would eventually reach the top. Over a period of time, his students realized there was no other way but to fall in line when it came to Prof. *Pranhachkal*.

His son, Karan, however, had started resenting his father's single-minded behaviour towards him. Often while sitting on the modest-sized kitchen *chowki*, a low dewan that served the purpose of a dinner table where the whole family sat together night after night, Papa would tell Karan how he could foresee the future for him. '*Bhagwan* has a grand design for you. I know you feel I'm being tough on you sometimes. You are not able to see the future, which is clearly visible to me. Your hard work will pay off one day when you crack the IAS.' Battling mixed emotions, he would say with a sense of pride in his voice, 'The first IAS officer in our entire family.' Sitting at the head of the table was Krishn Dhar, his father, who would often give out a deep sigh when he heard these words.

Krishn Dhar could see history repeating itself right in front of his eyes. He had struggled as a peon in a government office, where he was a nobody and remained a nobody throughout his career. His frustration at not providing enough for his family and more often than not, venting out his anger at little Pran and his timid, scared mother bothered him to no end. His career seemed to be jinxed, but he was hell-bent that his son would become a highly respected IAS officer, and Krishn Dhar's name would be taken with awe in the close-knit Pandit society.

Krishn Dhar was not aiming beyond his reach. His son was indeed an exceptionally intelligent and gifted child. He not only passed his junior school with top grades, but was good in sports too. His father was happy that he was showing a keen interest in science and mathematics, but disapproved of him spending his time on the cricket field. This disapproval soon turned into an obsession. By the time Pran Nath was in class 10, his father made sure that every waking moment after school was spent with his nose buried in his books. His mother was given strict instructions to monitor him, and the poor woman was never able to stand up for her son. There were times when Pran Nath would appeal to her, begging her to let him go to play. But even if she wanted to grant him that wish, she knew if her husband found out, he would be unforgiving.

Pran Nath got an opportunity to sneak out one evening when his mother had gone to the market to buy vegetables. What a stroke of luck! It was on the day his friends were playing the final against a rival team that was on a winning streak for the last many matches. His friend Shoukat, the captain, had discussed with him during recess at school earlier in the day about the need for a fast bowler like him in the team. Maybe, he'd get a chance to prove himself today. The match went on until late evening. Shoukat's team had amassed a respectable total of 220, but towards the fag end of the game, his worst fears were coming true. Just three overs remained and they still had three batsmen to bowl out. Meanwhile, the rival team was making steady progress at 210 runs. Pran Nath, who was earlier not sure whether Shoukat had noticed him in the crowd, jumped with joy when he was called to bowl. He was not happy with the first over, as the score had now reached 213. The next bowler was Aziz, who managed to give away just one run and picked up a wicket too! With just eight runs to win, the rival team's supporters were already celebrating with loud claps and chants. Pran Nath picked up a wicket on the first ball of the over and capped the win in the last ball. But all he remembered about that day throughout his life was the sting of a slap on his face, right there on the field, just as he had bowled the match-winning ball. His father's eyes were bloodshot with anger. He twisted Pran Nath's ear tightly and dragged him out of the field, mouthing expletives all the way home. The scars of the violence that he and his mother witnessed that day would stay with them forever.

Chapter 3

Krishn Dhar kept a tight leash on the activities of his son from that day onwards. However, Pran Nath's performance in school saw a steady dip. No matter how much time and energy his father put into forcing him to study, his interest in studies vaned by the day. As a result, he barely managed to pass his class 12 exams. All his father's dreams of him having a high-profile government position vanished into thin air. After graduation, he enrolled in the physics department of the University of Kashmir, and some aspects of his life that had given him comfort made a comeback. He left home, took up a room near the university and conducted tuitions for pocket money. He even joined the university cricket team. The high point of his cricketing life arrived when in the finals of the inter-college cricket tournament, he picked up the winning wicket of the Engineering College team, incidentally captained by Shoukat. This time around, he received pats on the back and shouts of 'Hip Hip Hooray,' and 'Pran our Hero,' could be heard from afar.

At that point in time, the desire to rebel against a tyrannical father was greater than to prove himself academically. As he grew free of his father's influence, regret slowly started to dawn on him. This was triggered when even after a decade of working as a lecturer at the university, his career had reached a plateau. The invigorating feeling he got at first in the classroom soon turned sour with the repetitive, dull and mundane routine. It took a long time for him to accept mediocrity as his middle name. As often happens with people who harbour bitterness and anger and want to hide it from the rest of the world, he turned controlling towards his family and his students alike. Karan, his son, was one who mostly bore the brunt of this side of his nature.

All his life, Pran Nath had held his father responsible for his failures and was intent on being firm with his son, but he never raised his hand or even his voice at any of the child's indiscretions. Karan would make his dream come true. He would be an IAS officer his father could never become, but it would be his own dream too. From a very tender age, the seed was sown in his mind. Pran Nath was confident that Karan had happily accepted it. His intelligent eyes would light up as his dad told him how bureaucrats were at the helm of every government policy. The high esteem they commanded and the name they made for themselves.

'*Sahib, Sahib che karan sari timan*, people run around calling them Sahib,' he would say.

Karan lapped it all up, yet watching his father with Sanjana, sometimes made him wish he would treat his son in the same manner.

Sanjana became his stress-buster from the day she came into the world. To his wife Sunita's surprise, Sanjana could easily disarm her rather rigid, unsmiling husband, with just a look. He adored her, spoilt her silly and would carry her around on his shoulders whenever they went out. Sanjana's world was full of her father's warmth. Her brother too would never leave her side. That day, sitting on that *chowki* in the kitchen, Papa was once again telling Karan how he was confident about him cracking the IAS exam.

Sanjana, who must have been around 14, couldn't help but ask, 'Papa, what about me? What will I be when I grow up?'

Taken aback, Papa had laughed at first. While feeding her a piece of fish that he had carefully deboned, he had whispered in her ear, 'My daughter, you will always remain my darling daughter.'

Sunita would watch the father-daughter duo from a distance. Sometimes, she would be struck with awe as she watched her husband smile at Sanjana. His voice sweetened and he would be completely relaxed. Those moments were only reserved for his little girl, never for his wife of so many years. '*Unpad*,' '*Gawar*,' illiterate and ignorant were the words she had heard often from him. He did not seem to notice her wince when he made fun of her in the presence of his parents. '*Sunitay akal badi ki bhens*? what is bigger, a brain or a buffalo?' he would chuckle. Although she chided herself for the thoughts, she had to admit that sometimes, she envied her daughter for having a part of her husband she was completely denied.

Chapter 4

In a couple of weeks, Karan would have his *mekhal* ceremony, one of the most important occasions in every Kashmiri Pandit young man's life – a ceremony commemorating his 'coming of age.' The whole family was engrossed in the arrangements. There would be a four-hour long pooja, followed by dinner for nearly 100 guests. Prof. Pran Nath had personally visited neighbours and relatives to invite them.

'How can we miss a treat of *dum aloo*?' quipped his close friend and neighbour Abdul Shaffaq, whose family had lived next door for generations.

Their bonding was well known in the Hindu and Muslim communities alike, not unlike any other in the Valley that thrived on mutual generosity and support.

'Let us know if you need anything at all, Pran *bhaisaahib*,' Shaffaq's wife Sakeena had said. She had visited them in the afternoon to help the rest of the ladies with the cleaning of the rice – a chore among many others that was required to be done at home, since the *wazwaan*, or the feast, would be cooked in the backyard, just adjoining the wall of the Shaffaq's garden, by professional Hindu cooks, the *wazas*.

A week from the ceremony, Pran Nath, felt the first ripples of an undercurrent of hostility amongst his own people. He had stepped out of his home to have a quick smoke on the roadside when a young boy got down from his motorcycle and approached him.

Hands on his hips, he glared at Pran Nath, and before he could react, the youngster slapped him on his head saying, '*Batta hachkala gasu wain dafa*. Leave, get lost!'

A visibly shaken Pran Nath received a phone call from Shaffaq that evening. 'Pranbhai, I've heard there have been riots in the nearby locality. Please, all of you stay indoors. Let's hope this dies down soon.'

He could sense the urgency in his friend's tone. The incident that had happened earlier that day, kept playing in his mind, unnerving him. His father too talked about communal tension in the neighbouring locality, where miscreants had thrown a petrol bomb at a Pandit's home. There was an eerie silence in the household as the children were sent to bed early and the elders kept vigil throughout the night.

His worst fears came true when Pran Nath found a piece of paper outside his gate which read 'PANDITS LEAVE KASHMIR WITHIN 24 HOURS OR DIE.' His whole body was shaking by now. For a while, he toyed with the idea that this was a prank. But deep down, he could sense the danger bells.

As he hurriedly entered the house, he overheard his father talking animatedly with his uncle, Shiv, over the phone. 'Do you think this is serious? Should we worry?'

Shiv Chacha, who was his father's younger brother, seemed very anxious indeed. He too had found a warning note outside his house that morning.

'Shiv is always prone to anxiety. He takes needless tension even when there is the minutest problem,' said his mother, in an effort to calm down her jittery nerves.

They spent the next hour trying to contact everyone they knew. What they found took away the earth under their feet. Many of their friends and relatives had already left or were packing their bags.

Shiv made another call to his elder brother. '*Bhaisahib*, let's leave while we can. No one will be able to stop the tsunami when it comes. It will take away everything; let's save the lives of our loved ones,' he said in a choked voice.

'This can't be true! This is our home too! Why should we leave? Who has the right to even say this to us?' Pran Nath was shouting now.

'*Beta*,' said his father, who was standing close by. Keeping one hand on his son's shoulder, he spoke calmly, 'These things have a way of dying down. They will realize their mistake very soon. Meanwhile, we can't put everyone's life in danger. Tell the womenfolk and kids to start packing. You and I must have a plan ready quickly.'

This had been the first time Papa had allowed himself to show some concern about Pran Nath ever since that fateful day at the cricket ground, when on one hand, he had secured victory for his team, and on the other, lost the trust of his father. They declined Shaffaq's offer to drive them to the nearest bus stand.

'Please pack only the necessary items,' Shaffaq advised, while his wife comforted Pran Nath's family with kind and reassuring words. 'It's just for a day or two, you will see.' Hugging Karan she smiled and said, 'I am going to wear a *sharara* at your *mekhal* ceremony. It's all going to be fine.'

Not one person in the entire populace of the cursed Valley could envisage what happened next. A small trickle of families huddled in groups heading towards an unknown destination, soon turned into thousands of people, all jostling for a seat in any bus, truck or car that would take them beyond the Jawahar tunnel on the Jammu-Kashmir highway, far from the horrors that their homeland was being systematically subjected to. The centuries-old social fabric that the ancient Hindu, Islamic and Sufi mystics had weaved with compassion, wisdom and love, was, within a few days, torn into fragments and splattered with the blood of the innocent.

For the majority of those fleeing, this was the first time they were ever venturing out of the city or village. They had hardly felt the need. Families, indeed the entire neighbourhood, would readily support each other in good and bad times alike. Maybe, this was one reason why they thought this would pass soon, and they would be back home, back to normal in no time. Little did they know that the cruel wind of time would blow them far away from their beloved motherland like the seeds of the Kikar tree. Many would die with an unanswered prayer to visit their home. Others would try to sew together whatever was left of their tattered lives. But all would suffer, the ones that left and the ones that were left behind.

Chapter 5

Shiv had taken Sanjana's grandparents with him to stay with his in-laws in Chandigarh. A distant cousin of Sanjana's father, Aditya, had insisted the rest of the family stay with him in Jammu. They lived in his small house for almost a year after their departure from Kashmir.

'Let go off yesterday; it is gone,' were the words that many books and gurus advised to a mind haunted by time's relentless, merciless blows. But for Sanjana, whose peace of mind was forever taken away ever since her brother Karan had died, it was not something she could let go of easily. Visions of a speeding truck hitting him with a loud thud, his blood-curdling scream and her own body that had suddenly seemed to have turned into a lead statue, haunted her.

Sanjana sought refuge in a corner just outside the tiny kitchen. She, however, was not alone there. An old lady with an ancient face, a frail frame and vacant eyes, kept her company. She first thought her to be Uncle Aditya's mother, but later learnt that she had been separated from her family while they fled the Valley, and had somehow ended up here. Not any different from her own self, Sanjana often thought, for after the terrible accident, a part of her was permanently cut from her family and there was no one to rescue her.

'Maaf gasi karun. Bhagwan kari soruy theek. Seek forgiveness. God will help you,' she had whispered in Sanjana's ear.

The old lady and Sanjana were shelling peas that afternoon. She had absentmindedly put a few peas in her mouth when her mother had rather angrily snatched the bowl of peas from her.

'Maaf gasi karun,' the old lady had said because she understood.

Forgive whom? Herself? She was the one who had been obstinate and thrown a tantrum because she was hungry. She had begged Karan to cross the road to get her some biscuits. Papa had volunteered to go, but Karan being Karan, had already left before he could say anything. It was just the way he was. Always caring; always the first to help. No, there was no way she could forgive herself.

But time and again she did seek forgiveness from her parents. With folded hands, she had asked for their forgiveness. She touched their feet and wept tears of desperation but they did not budge.

Something familiar had tugged at Pran Nath's heart for a moment when his daughter had fallen at his feet, trembling and weeping. She had called him 'Papaji,' just as she would in those endearing times when she was little and sat in his lap all the time.

But her words, '*maaf kardo na*...please forgive me,' had jolted him back to reality.

He simply couldn't come to terms that Karan was gone forever, and so had the little girl who reigned over his heart. Her father had shut the door of his room on her face. She sat on the floor near the door many a night, apologizing again and again. It seemed to her the doors of her parent's hearts were permanently shut to her.

Pran Nath had suddenly seemed to have aged by a decade. His gait was slower, his voice lower. He, who had not so long ago been a workaholic, a stickler for rules and discipline, soon became a shadow of his former self. The horrors of the past months were continuously playing on his mind. They became an excuse to drift away from the present. He became quiet and withdrawn, having thrown himself at the mercy of his fate.

His wife, on the other hand, realized very quickly that if they didn't do something about their situation, it would get worse. She needed to step up. They couldn't live at the mercy of relatives forever. She had to find work soon to get their lives back on track. Sunita, who, until recently, did not have an inkling about how the outside world functioned, had jumped into the arena. But she soon found that there were thousands of scavengers like her, looking for odd jobs. Sunita let go of her vanity and would not refuse, even if there were tiny scraps to be found. For just 10 rupees, she would give a good oil massage to the wealthy ladies living in big *kothis* in Gandhi Nagar. As she got introduced to more households, she would help with domestic work during occasions and also babysit. She was on the lookout for a job for Sanjana too.

A day came when 16-year-old Sanjana was unceremoniously sent to a tennis academy as a cleaner. She would have a mop and a broom in her hands throughout the day, cleaning smelly locker rooms and filthy toilets. On the first day, as she left home, she had looked back, hoping to see her father, who surely would have argued with her mother to at least look for something better for her, but he had not come out of his room. The next ten months were a blur in her memory. Depressing work, rude and callous academy kids, co-workers who didn't give a damn and the brutal weather of Jammu, made her life miserable.

Tennis happened by chance. She had jokingly fielded a few balls at one of the trainers one morning. Kartik Sir had found her swing interesting. This was the first time she had held a racket TO play, but he had sensed her naturalness. She had a powerful arm too. Kartik Sir especially came an hour earlier every day just to practice with her. Within six months, he knew he hadn't wasted his time, for Sanjana was a quick learner. What he did not know was that the power in her swing came from within. Months of pent-up anger and frustration were being dissipated every time she lifted her arm to play. He even nicknamed her *'hatodi,'* the hammer.

Within a year, her enthusiastic trainer announced to her parents that he had found a prodigy in her. He wanted her to train full-time, free of cost, and play for the regional and hopefully national levels. Her mother, although reluctant at first, finally relented, and the following year, Sanjana buried herself in the busy life of tennis practice, thankful to finally get a respite from the waves of rejection and pain that had threatened to engulf her life.

Chapter 6

Vineet had always found Jammu to be rather dull and boring. This year too he had resisted when his parents planned their annual 'pilgrimage' from Houston to their hometown. The only silver lining being the week or at the most ten days, he got to spend with his cousins in Bombay. Its glittering streets and the heady nightlife were still in his head as he stepped onto the tennis court that day and confronted an opponent who knocked the daylight off him. She hit the ball hard and fast. He struggled to keep up with her lightning-like footwork. She had her eyes only on the ball. The game was over even before it began. She simply turned away and left without giving him a second glance.

He came back for more and lost every single time. Who would have thought the little urchin was so tough? Vineet had been playing tennis ever since he was six, and was rather proud of his achievements in school and college. Winning was a habit for him. But this was a different ball game altogether. No matter how much he studied her game, he couldn't figure out what made her tick. She had begun to terrify him. He had started to have restless nights where all he was thinking of was how to outsmart her.

Vineet had arrived at the tennis court early one hot August morning and watched Sanjana play with Kartik.

'She's good, isn't she?' Kartik had asked Vineet, who couldn't keep his eyes off her.

'As good as a champ!' he had replied.

He'd walked up to Sanjana and shook her hand. 'Hi again. I'm a big fan.'

'Thank you,' was all she could muster.

Sanjana was rather shy around Vineet. He was much older than her and looked like a model. When he walked up casually to her for a chat, she would struggle for words. He was the only person apart from Kartik Sir who had shown any interest in her, and she liked that about him.

She had surprised herself when she agreed to go for coffee with him. The tiny cafe just outside the academy was not very fancy, but she didn't care. That evening had had a cathartic effect on her. She had poured out her heart to this complete stranger, who had looked at her as if he understood her well. She giggled at his jokes and laughed when he mimicked the funny accent of his cousins. He took her to movies and restaurants. She would sneak out to meet him, bunk training and lie through her teeth about her whereabouts.

Within a month, Vineet had asked her to come to America with him, as his wife. There was nothing better she wanted than to get away, far away from the drudgery of her life in Jammu, far away from the accusing looks of her father and the icy glare of her mother.

PART 2

Chapter 1

Sanjana was hovering around the closed door for a long time, hoping it would open and she would get a glimpse of her youngest daughter, Kia. But it remained shut throughout the day.

'She must be exhausted,' said Mummy.

'*Guadde kya osuk pahadan khasun?* what was the need to climb those mountains?' she asked and then she chuckled at a memory, '*waise chas be ti Shankracharya khachmiz schoolas manz*, for your information, I too have climbed the Shankracharya Hill when I was in school. *Waahay kot gayi tyim doh*,' she lamented about the days, whose mere memory would act as a balm on her tortured soul.

Whatever had happened to her days? Sanjana asked herself. What a fool she had been, thinking that she could escape her destiny so easily. Vineet had not pressured her to marry him; it was she who was in a hurry to leave, to escape reality. It was very clear from the beginning that Vineet had just wanted to present a ready-made servant to his parents – a servant who would forever be obliged to him for giving her a lease of life, a slave who would never be able to rebel. Domesticity was subtly forced on her, and soon, became her second nature. She would spend her days cooking and cleaning the tiny house she lived in with Vineet and his parents and the motel they owned. She was required to look after their every need without asking for much in return. She remained cut off from her family in India, except for a customary phone call every month when Vineet made sure she spoke the right words only. She often heard her own voice in her head, the words long lost in time, asking her doting father, the centre of her universe, "*What about me? What will I be when I grow up?*"

Sanjana remembered when Sonal and Mahi were born just a year apart; it was the only time in her married life that she was genuinely happy. "*Fatherhood would possibly change the way Vineet behaved towards me,*" she had hoped. But, his disdain for her was obvious to the extent that he refused to even talk to her unless necessary. Their daughters brought back the laughter in the house, but Sanjana was rarely a part of it. She remained a mute spectator, when with time, like the rest of the family, her daughters too learnt to take her for granted.

When after a gap of 10 years of Mahi's birth, she learnt that she was pregnant again, her whole being was filled with regret and sadness. She had worked very hard to turn herself into as emotionless as possible. A dead woman walking. Bringing another life into her dismal world seemed depressing. She wished she had died instead of her grandfather when she got the news from India. Though full of trepidation, she took that flight.

The reception she got was expected of course, given that she had come without her husband and daughters.

There were no tears of welcome or any pampering. Her father did not lower the wall of silence between them, and her mother only softened a little once she found that Sanjana was pregnant.

Sanjana was, in a way, relieved that no one asked her about her life in Houston. She spent the time in Delhi taking long walks alone, or sleeping for hours. She would often stroll past the tennis academy, and one day, mustered enough courage to step inside. When she saw the unmistakable figure of her tennis coach, Kartik Sir, she couldn't control her tears. He watched her from a distance, came running to her and hugged her. That moment saw a dam break inside her. Shivering and stuttering, she managed to say the words she had wanted to say to him for a long time, 'I'm sorry.'

Ignoring Vineet's calls that hovered from angry threats to plain hostility, she decided to have her baby in Delhi. It was a girl. Kia's presence in her life started to thaw the coldness that seemed to have made a permanent place in her. She would look at her with wonder, as if she had never had babies before. She talked to her all the time. She would tell baby Kia about her brave uncle Karan and her loving grandparents. 'Kia, you will love tennis. You will be a star one day. I just know it.'

The decision to leave Kia behind was probably the best decision of her life, Sanjana thought. Her parents, although surprised, couldn't hide their delight. It was as if a ray of light had entered their empty lives. She made occasional visits, always alone. Kia was nurtured and cherished by her grandparents. The day she joined formal school was also her first day at the tennis academy. Her grandfather personally took her to practice tennis every day. Her grandmother showered her with love and attention. At 15, Kia was a budding tennis champion. She was tall, attractive, witty and outgoing. Her laughter and twinkling eyes filled many hearts with delight. Yet, when it came to her mother, her demeanour changed. She would clamp up and withdraw into a fortress of her thoughts, one which her mother could not enter. This time was no different. The moment she heard that her mother was visiting, Kia took off to Kasol on a solitary trek. She was hoping her mother would be gone before she returned. Her Nationals were starting in a few weeks and despite her reluctance, she had to return soon as she could no longer miss her tennis practice.

Kia's best friend Samara lived just a few houses down the lane. Kia's grandmother had been fascinated by Samara's long silky hair and porcelain skin.

'You are just like your mother,' she had said many a time, adding with a smile, 'Aren't you lucky to inherit your dad's height?' a polite way of saying thank God you didn't get his not-so-flattering features. Kia protected Samara from such jibes, for her own childhood got a semblance of normalcy at Samara's house, where she spent a considerable amount of time. Her dad, who she called Doctor Uncle, loved gardening and would take a lot of pride in growing all sorts of exotic plants in his tiny front lawn.

'My little patch is nothing like what your grandfather must have had in Kashmir. I'm sure that must have been really grand,' he would say.

She loved to go to their house on Sundays when her mother used to bake cakes and grill chicken. Samara had no sibling, and when she used to insist that Kia stay the night at her place, Kia would readily agree. In time, Kia's feelings turned towards envy. She tried to wrestle with those thoughts often, telling herself that maybe it was because of Samara's good looks and the attention she got from boys. Deep down, she knew that wasn't really what was making her feel bad. The expression of warmth on the faces of the three, Samara, her mother and her father when they were together, bothered her.

Her blood would boil when she thought of how her own parents had abandoned her. She had never met her father and her mother, yes, she was the one who was most responsible for her suffering. What kind of woman leaves her new born? Was it because she was the third daughter? Did she want a boy? Most probably, there was no place for a baby in her well-organized life where her two elder daughters and doting husband demanded every moment of her time. "*How engrossed she must be with her other daughters,*" she thought bitterly.

And now, she was here yet again. "*What does she expect from me?*" Kia had been fuming ever since she had heard her mother was going to be in town. She decided to stay out of her sight as much as she could.

A knock at her door. Sanjana stood there with a tennis racket in her hand, unrecognizable in shorts and a T-shirt. She walked up to her daughter and said, 'Come, let's have a match.'

Sanjana took one last look behind, before entering Terminal 3 at the international airport, Delhi. She stood there hesitant, forlorn. Her eyes, which were blurred with tears, couldn't believe what they saw next. Kia was running up to her. In a moment, she was hugging her tightly. They held each other for a long time. Laughing and crying at the same time, it was as if two halves of a whole had suddenly found each other.

'Mum,' the prodigal daughter said, at last. 'Mum, take care.'

'Take care, my sweetheart. I love you,' replied the mother who had suddenly found the universe in her lap.

THE END

VOICE

'What Were You Doing?'

It's my feeling that the ringtone of my new mobile phone, the one that took me a good 15 minutes to decide upon from dozens of choices, had somehow crawled into my body and had started to live along with my muscles, nerves and bones. For every time my phone came to life, I could feel a slight tingling in my body at first, then a deep hum would settle in, which could be felt for a long time after the phone shut up. It was as if the living entity inside me had finally taken charge, and with its uncontrolled treble, was definitely making merry at the expense of my peace of mind. I would have this urge to pull off my hair or just leave for some faraway place, never to come back home or better still, jump in the Dal Lake.

Once, I even switched it off, patting my back for such a smart move. But a moment after that, the landline started ringing. From the first ring, I could make out who it was. I could recognize Salim Beig's call from wherever I was in the world. There are times I ask the Almighty during my prayers what he was thinking when he made this person who opens every conversation with *'Kya osuk karan*? What were you doing?' What does he do with the information? But this much I can say with confidence; he needs to know every detail of my day (and sometimes night). My daily dose of whereabouts, what I ate, who I spoke to, whether I'm asleep or awake, whether I like what's happening with the government/media/neighbours/anyone and everyone, the most nondescript details of my everyday life, were like air and water to him – the very things keeping him alive.

'*Tal sa tulus wayn becharas*, why don't you pick up the phone and talk to the poor fellow,' my wife of 50 years urged. Zubeida had been hovering around, hoping I would just finish off the customary talking and buy some temporary peace of mind for at least a while. The tone of her voice meant that she was on the brink of losing her patience, and that meant borderline trouble for me. A big sigh and I picked up the call.

'*Kya sa osuk karan*? What were you doing?'

'I heard there is a leopard roaming around?' I don't know why I said that. Maybe I wanted to scare him out of his wits.

'*Kya sa chuk wanan*. What are you saying?' I could sense him getting alert.

'Didn't you hear the wailing of the dogs last night? The leopard has killed three dogs, that too of good breeds.'

His breathing quickened. 'Why are you scaring me?'

'*Cheyen drey*. I swear by you. There is a leopard roaming around in our locality. So, stay indoors. Don't even venture into your garden,' I said.

'But, but...'

My satisfaction deepened as I felt his breath quicken. I left his 'buts' hanging in the air and turned off the volume of my phone.

Salim Beig made his presence felt in my life only after we were both retired from our respective government jobs. My plans for my 'sunset years' were to slow down the hectic pace of life and live a peaceful life. Coming to think of it, after 15 years of retirement, I still think I should have at least discussed with Zubeida my perception of a 'peaceful life.' Sometimes, I feel she mistook the meaning as 'pieces of peace and full of war.' Conversations with Salim Beig did not help my situation either. No matter how well my day had gone, he would bring it down with his overly pessimistic and critical analysis, tearing down every simple incident, good or bad, into a series of horrors.

I had got a taste of his temperament a long time ago when we were representing our respective departments at a meeting with the Finance Minister. He had taken umbrage at my remark of not stretching the motions beyond what was there on the agenda.

'Sir, will you tell this person not to teach us the rules!' he had shouted, finger pointed in my direction.

The minister, however, was not amused and had asked him to restrain himself. But he kept arguing about the unfairness of my demands. My assistant, Shafiq, had labelled him a '*kaek,*' a Kashmiri word that has no equivalent in English, but 'wet blanket'/'garrulous' come close. Two decades later, he was the same, wearing the '*kaek*' badge with pride.

'*Kya sa osuk karan*? So, what are you up to now?'

It had been a week since the fictional leopard had roamed our streets and backyards. Salim Beig, who lived a few houses away, had kept watch every day till late evening.

Every morning, I would receive his call with the words, '*Shukr*, the leopard hasn't entered my property. Otherwise, who knows what would have happened!'

The past week had challenged my imagination to the limits. His excitement knew no bounds when I convinced him that our neighbour's ferocious Alsatian had been dragged by the leopard to some faraway place in the forests. He seemed disappointed when the next day I reported that the dog had miraculously escaped and had found its way back.

'Maybe it's a jackal,' he said.

'What are you talking about? A jackal is no match to a full-grown Alsatian,' I shot back. 'In fact, Jeela the compounder saw him dragging the poor dog. Do you know how many stitches the dog got?' I said, further spinning my tale of awe and terror.

I discovered tales like these kept his mind busy and away from the more ominous topics like 'do you think there will be a storm tonight?' that he was fond of first laying threadbare and then fretting about for a long time.

I remember, when one morning he had asked me the same question and I had answered, 'What makes you think there is going to be a storm? It's a perfectly beautiful day, clear skies.'

Pat came the reply, 'Don't you read the newspaper? The storm is definitely coming. Our garden will be flooded. There is going to be lightning too. I had told my gardener to cut the tall fir trees in the backyard, but he never listens. Now, lightning will strike them; there may even be a fire. Do you know the number of the fire station?'

Nevertheless, there were a few thundershowers that night, but Salim Beig kept me on high alert until midnight, just in case lightning strikes one of his tall fir trees and burns down his house.

It all started with what looked like a cry for help. Salim Beig had singled me out from thousands of his contacts to unburden his woes. He needed a shoulder to cry on, and I must say I was flattered at first. One of our first conversations was about his son Zubair, who had accepted a lucrative job offer in the US.

'He could have made more money dealing with Kashmiri handicrafts,' he lamented.

'But he's a banker. And starting a business from scratch is not so easy. Besides, he has no background in business, leave alone handicrafts,' I replied.

'Oh, he could have worked for J&K Bank. They would have been happy to take him in.'

'But he has got his dream placement. Are you complaining because you don't want him to leave your side?'

'No. No. He has to settle down too. Do you think he will marry an American?'

'Let him go first. We will cross the bridge when we reach it.'

He had wanted to discuss this further, but was rather unhappy with my responses as I kept discouraging him from further speculation of Zubair's tryst with an American girl, losing touch with his family here in Kashmir and completely turning into an 'American'.

'They are not zombies. Even if he does become an "American," they don't have horns on their heads,' I had retorted.

Salim Beig was not really the kind of person I would be friends with. At first, I felt his obsessive habit of calling me at any time of the day or night was irritating. Here was one specimen of the most extraordinary kind. Anyone will tell you about the way of life of a common Kashmiri. They thrive on interaction with all and sundry - neighbours, relatives, friends and foes alike. To keep themselves updated, giving their opinion or free advice, they have no qualms at dropping in at any given time unannounced anywhere, be it to chat with a random shopkeeper (a butcher is a favourite), or a far-off cousin, even if it means driving hours to reach their house. Meeting each other on every occasion is on the daily calendar. Births, deaths and weddings apart, occasions like children passing exams (10th and 12th and medical and engineering seats) call for huge celebrations. They throng in dozens along with their families and even kids in tow to visit an ailing patient at home or hospital.

But here was a rare Kashmiri who was getting his daily dose about what was happening in the outside world through another person, that too without stepping out of his front yard. The last time he had ventured out of his house was once a long time ago, to see me off till the main road, about 100 metres from his gate. He himself had admitted that the experience had left him dizzy.

'*Gyure hasa aam*, my head is spinning,' was his explanation of leaving me abruptly and hurrying back home.

'Your relatives must be calling you names; you never pay them any attention,' I had said.

'*Cheyt cham*! I'll be damned! I tried to ask about their well-being on the phone, but they don't take kindly to my calls!'

This is when he revealed that he had zeroed on to me as his agony aunt/friend/philosopher/guide after sieving through a plethora of relatives and acquaintances. Many of them took his calls just to be polite. He has no clue as to why so many of them just dropped him from their radar, some even going to the extent of blocking him. My guess was that they were smarter than me. Well, I didn't know whether to be pleased or furious. But somehow, he seemed to be mighty relieved to have found someone at the other end of the phone who had the patience to go through his whining without wanting to end the agony by either shooting him or themselves.

I must admit, at times, these conversations often provided much-needed entertainment on a dull day. Also, with time, I likened myself to a philanthropist. After all, I was helping someone in need.

'*Kale dod!* A headache!' exclaimed my wife, when I had arrived at the conclusion that I was Salim Beig's anchor, and where would he be without me? Zubeida's frustration was unfounded. But I completely ignored the sarcasm when she said, '*Dil ko behlane ke liye Galib ye khayal accha hai*, You are just kidding yourself.'

It was the cricket season and the TV, transistor and generator had my complete attention. Yes, it's 2022, and the world has forgotten about the radio, but my old faithful transistor serves as a good backup if, during a cricket match, electricity snaps and the generator fails. Cricket is what I completely worship. Ideally, I don't want to miss a single minute. So, my schedule is set accordingly. No travelling or even going out for a chore. Sometimes, when the excitement gets too high, Zubeida insists on checking my BP and pulse. But the TV cannot be switched off even if my BP is hitting the roof. Also, the cricket season is when Alexander Bell is cursed the most for inventing the phone. For Salim Beig has this compulsive need to discuss every ball with me. The irony is, he cannot tell cricket from soccer, and he is clueless about the teams, the players or the place the match is taking place in. But he has me. It's like when Edmund Hilary was asked why he climbed Everest, his reply was, 'Because it's there.' He didn't get the game, but I discovered he had this eerie knack to predict the score. How he did it was beyond my understanding. But he was fairly accurate in predicting sudden twists in the game. When he spoke in favour of my favourite team, I would happily chat with him for the next few days, which was like a reward for him. But he was also responsible for a near heart attack.

Once, when I was snug in the feeling that today was a good day, as everything was going smoothly, he started talking about seeing dark clouds outside his window.

'It might rain. What happens to the game if it rains?'

I laughed and said, 'The match is in Melbourne; not in your backyard.'

'But what will happen if it rains there?'

'Why will it rain? It's a clear day,' I said irately.

'No, but if it rains will they have to abandon the game? It's a pity because India has a huge total, and as you said, their fast bowlers are in form. So, they will win then?'

'Of course, the match is in their pocket. Do you have any doubts?'

'Only if it doesn't rain.'

I had a smug smile on. He was losing his touch, I felt. But sure enough, an hour later, the drizzling started in the Melbourne Cricket Ground where India was making mincemeat of the Aussies. Six of their wickets had already gone. Indian bowlers were having a field day. There was no way Australia could match India's highest-ever ODI score. The slight drizzling took a few seconds to become a huge downpour. Everyone was caught off guard, and so was I. More curses to Alexander Graham Bell.

With time, I turned into a doctor/lawyer/counsellor/political, sports, and entertainment news analyst to Salim Beig. With every session with him, I felt I was getting better with my voice modulation, sprinkling of laughter, sarcasm and sadness. I was like an interactive radio with just one listener.

'*Syun kya osvu*? What was for dinner?'

'Zubeida outdid herself today. I'd got 5 kg of fish, fresh from the Dal. Just three big ones. She made two dishes, one with lotus stem and the other with radish. She also fried some pieces for me. She knows I like fried fish.' I said in my best teasing voice. I could sense his mouth-watering since he was quiet for a few moments.

'Are there such large fish in the Dal?'

'Of course, there are. Leave your house and walk near the banks of the Dal. There are a few fisherwomen ready with their catch early morning.'

'I think you are exaggerating. The fish in Dal are not that big,' he argued. 'I don't even bother to get fish,' lied the man who wouldn't step out of the comfort of his house even if he was dying. 'Dilafroz can never match Bhabhiji in cooking fish,' he finally declared.

Grapes are sour, I thought. His wife, Dilafroz, was never good enough at anything, according to him. The one time I had visited him, she had laid out a scrumptious breakfast. *Shammi kebabs*, homemade *parathas*, eggs and Kashmiri *chai*, all freshly made and delicious. But Salim Beig had not been happy.

'We should have had *bakarkhani* with nun chai. Why are the kebabs so bland?' he had complained.

This may be one of the reasons for his dry take on blessings bestowed on us by Allah, I concluded. He was full of scorn and criticism. He had deliberately deprived himself of many simple pleasures of life, I had pointed out.

'Oh! Is it? I haven't noticed,' he replied with a hint of a smile.

Salim Beig had two large wall clocks prominently displayed on a wall in the living room of his house. They were a gift from me actually. He had been really fixated on knowing the time in America after his only son left to settle there. No matter how much I educated him about the time difference between California and Srinagar, he refused to learn, simply because calling up and asking me was better than calculating it himself. Eventually, I sent the two wall clocks, one showing the time in Srinagar and the other in California. It was another thing that he would call to ask whether it was day or night there.

We talked about death one day. I was rather surprised by the way he spoke, straight and matter-of-factly.

He even sounded poetic. 'There would be no bigger relief than the bounty of death from life's miseries.'

It so happened that the very next day, I had to be hospitalized for severe stomach pain. Zubeida had received his call and informed him that I might have to undergo surgery for gallbladder removal. She told me that he had remained silent for a long time. I did not hear from him for several days even after returning home from the hospital. I was angry. He didn't even care enough to ask about my well-being! A week went by, and my phone was yet to display his name. I found myself looking at it in amazement. The ringtone that had entered my bloodstream had made me an addict! I became restless and irritable. Zubeida passed the phone to me during one such episode which she was quick to point out as my 'withdrawal symptom.'

'Call him and get on with life,' she sighed.

THE END

QUICKSAND

Chapter 1

This was the first time she had kept me waiting. As I sat on the dirty grey stone steps on the banks of the Dal, I carefully scanned the entire lake for a long time. A couple of fishing boats were idling away, but none of them was the blue one my eyes were looking for. I tried once again to reassure myself by touching the crisp paper in my jacket pocket. My shoulders were tightening up, indicating the start of a migraine, a dreadful thought. I hurriedly rolled my scarf and tied it around my forehead to prevent the throbbing pain from spreading. The empty silence on the Boulevard was being slowly breached by heavily loaded SUVs speeding towards Sonamarg and beyond. Dawn was yet to break, and this was the best time to beat the traffic and the army convoys enroute to Ladakh.

I sat there for a long time, conversations with Ayesha running several times in my mind. "*What is it that she didn't understand? Hadn't I been the only one to hear her out? How many hours I had spent trying to figure out a way for her to escape the drudgery of her existence! What a pity,*" I sighed. To my mind, that was the only way my thoughts could travel, refusing to tread to places where there would be more complex questions and even more impossible answers. Anger and disbelief were heating up my throbbing head now. The piece of paper was a ticket to her freedom. An air ticket that would have taken her far away, at last, to have a life of peace. One last glance to scan the darkness before me and I walked briskly towards my house.

My routine, which had been almost regimental until that day, had been hard hit by the change in plans. My rattled mind struggled to take control. The morning tea was getting late. I had forgotten to wake up Kaka, and that meant breakfast would be late too. Kaka would be lucky if he was able to get the *rotis* from the neighbouring *kandur* this late. I hurriedly kept the water for boiling, and calling Kaka to keep an eye on it, rushed to the *kandur*. By the time I was back, the sight of the mess in the kitchen gave me relief. It meant that Parvez and his mother had got their tea.

Kaka was sitting on the steps that led to the kitchen garden, holding a steaming glass of tea in the sleeves of his *pheran*. He looked up in disdain as I approached. I always suspected him of secretly smoking weed at night, for he looked like a *shoda*, a stoned person every morning. Always unkept and slow to follow any instructions. In any case, he would work at his pace, no matter how much I tried telling him to hurry up. Having been in this household even before I arrived, he had made it clear from the beginning that he had every right to do his work without taking instructions from anyone, me in particular.

'Didn't you keep any tea for me?' I asked.

I wasn't surprised when he shrugged. 'I thought you had *chai* earlier.'

Fuming, I said, 'If you are done, cut onions and chillies for omelettes. Breakfast is getting late.'

It was like any other day. Yet, I felt it to be just a little more unsettling. Parvez complained throughout the morning of my inability to prioritise my housework and schedule.

'There cannot be one woman in Kashmir as lazy as you,' he had taunted.

Ammaji wanted to know when I was planning to get her suit from the tailor. She wanted to wear it to her daughter's housewarming dinner tonight. I must have called Ahadjoo at least ten times yesterday, but he had argued that I was confused about the delivery date. It would be ready only next week. Ammaji did not keep her voice low when she called her sister to complain about how I had deliberately not gotten the suit from the tailor.

'*Ye lavi na kunyi*, she is worthless,' she spat on the phone.

She did not mention that I was not considered worthy enough to be invited to Shazia's new home. As I held my painful head and fought waves of nausea, I scolded myself for not having a plan B.

It was Shazia who had first asked me to be her sister-in-law. 'Think of how much fun it will be. We will live in the same house and do whatever we want. Parvez Bhaijan never minds about anything I do. He is so easy-going and generous. I'm sure Mummy will love you since you are also my best friend,' she had gushed while we shared a cold drink at the Women's College canteen.

Parvez would have been a catch had I been interested in marriage. Shazia came from a wealthy family. They had a three-storey house in Rajbagh with a huge garden and several cars. What Parvez lacked in the looks department, he made up with his costly clothes and flamboyant lifestyle. He would drive up to the college sometimes to pick up or drop Shazia, and that was the time a lot of girls would be evaluating the prospects of spending the rest of their days with him by their side.

That was nearly two decades back. At that time, getting married was last on my list of priorities. I had seen many marriages at close quarters festering with time. A classmate, Sheenu, was the first to jump on the bandwagon when she was merely 17. She was from a well-to-do family. I mostly got a complex from her pretty looks. It came as a surprise when we heard she had got married even before the first-year results were out. I was secretly delighted to have her out of my sight. Although the girls who had attended her wedding talked about her designer dress and jewellery for days, I knew she would be soon overburdened with housework and kids. About five years after she got married, I saw Sheenu buying shoes for her toddler. She ignored me. Gone were the stylish dresses, the fresh looks and the painted nails. She looked drab. I felt sorry for her.

My aunt, Sabiha Khala, too had got married in her teens. She completed her MBBS after marriage. The demanding job of a gynaecologist and looking after the household, the in-laws, three kids and a very possessive husband took a huge toll on her health. She died at the age of 35, just after giving birth to a son.

A relative from my mother's side, Biba, used to visit us often. She was ancient, had a hunch back and wrinkles all over her face and hands. I remember her twinkling eyes and toothless grin. She used to insist on hugging me tightly and planting wet kisses all over my face. I used to find her quite disgusting, especially since she used to have a strange odour, which I have since associated with old people. I later found out that she had studied law and also had a double MA degree! When I was around 10, she entered my room one day and took my hand. We crossed the long veranda into the front garden, which had beautiful flowers in neat beds, a burst of subtle sunshine and a cool breeze.

'*Yuth doh cha zaaye karan*? Why waste such a lovely day,' she whispered.

I remember her noisily sipping her *nun chai* while wolfing down chunks of plum cake. Caressing my hair, she had said that I reminded her of my mother, her most favourite niece. She hoped I would grow up to be as vivacious and full of life as her.

'Her laughter could be heard from the street outside,' she said.

The pride she took in her newly constructed house, which was actually an 8-bedroom mansion gifted to her by her father, was talked about long after she passed. The excitement in the household could not be contained when I arrived after two miscarriages. She had ordered my clothes, toys and accessories from abroad. I had a specially made bathtub before anyone had heard about it in Kashmir. I also had a pram and a highchair. My first birthday was nothing short of a dream, she told me.

'*Magar badkismat aes bichar*, how unfortunate she was. She did not live to see your second birthday.'

That was the first time anyone had told me about my mother. Biba had promised me that she would hunt for the picture she had of my mother as a bride and get it for me on her next visit.

I later learnt that my father hadn't even waited a year before remarrying my beautiful and stylish stepmother who was fifteen years his junior. He was completely besotted with her. He would often go on long business trips taking her along while keeping me in the care of servants. She showed no interest in the household. I could mostly see her in the evening sometimes when she had either entered the home after spending time with her friends or was leaving for a party. I would sometimes spy on her putting on her makeup. Her high coiffure and bangs fascinated me. She wore tight-fitting shirts without slits on the sides that made her look like a curvaceous film star.

My childhood has been a blur. Although I was living in the same house, I was kept in a separate wing with a garrulous nanny to take care of me. I met my father only on rare occasions like Eid. He never hugged me. I was asked to join for the customary lunch, given *Eidi* and sent off to my side of the house. I had spied on him playing with his young sons and chatting animatedly with my stepmother. Many years later, I had mustered some courage and asked him, as he lay on his deathbed, why he had kept himself away from me when I was just an infant.

He had replied, looking directly at me, 'Every time I saw your face, I was reminded of how your mother died. I loved her a lot. The doctors had told her not to conceive after she had two miscarriages, but she was adamant. She died of complications she got during your birth, two painful years later.'

I had looked at his face for a long time. He looked pained and distraught. I believed him and carried on the guilt of killing my mother for a long, long time.

Chapter 2

I envied Ayesha, for her days and nights were uncomplicated. A tiny boat, a little bigger than a bathtub was her home. A handful of utensils, some small jars, a stove and a large can of water took up most of the space. A dirty rug was spread on its floor. Even a coop of hens could be found somewhere in the back of the boat. The boat was covered with plastic sheets.

I had met Ayesha while walking down the Boulevard one autumn morning nearly two years back. She had been sitting precariously on the brink of the boat while shouting expletives. '*Machar chui? geur tultham* Have you lost your mind? You are driving me crazy.'

I could see a fully grown hen, her brilliant red and white feathers agitatedly flapping in the wind while running from one end of the shore and back. Shrieking at the top of her voice, she was obviously in distress.

I had stopped to enquire from the woman. 'Has someone stolen her eggs?'

While tying a headscarf, she said, '*Amis che na pooeth ravmith*. She has lost her kids. She is like a mother to those ducklings over there.' In the deep end of the lake, I could see half a dozen ducklings, ignoring the pleas of their foster mom to come back. 'She worries about them whenever they get into the water,' she laughed, '*Bechar*, she thinks they will drown.'

I found the whole scene so endearing that I too sat there for a while to sympathise with the poor hen on the verge of a nervous breakdown.

The woman held out a broken cup with pink salty tea inside. I didn't have the heart to refuse. She talked about her silly hen for a while, her voice jovial, at the same time doing other chores too: cleaning dishes in the dirty water of the lake, folding clothes and keeping them in a small bucket. It was her slow drawl that caught my attention

'You don't speak like a Kashmiri,' I asked suddenly.

She was taken aback for a while. '*Poz hai chu*. Yes. True. I'm actually from Bihar.'

Surprised, I looked at her closely. The white headscarf, the printed *pheran* and a black faded *salwar* were typical of a *hyeanz* woman, the clan of fisherwomen. The face and mannerisms too had merged perfectly into the canvas of the small population of the people living in boats scattered around the many lakes in the vicinity. However, it was the slight tilt of the words that gave her away, something that did not fit.

'*Accha?*' I gasped.

'*Han, Hum Bihar se hain. Patna se*, I'm a Bihari from Patna,' she said in Hindi. 'Had you met me 10 years back, you wouldn't have recognised me. My name was

Jina before marriage. My husband changed it to Ayesha.' Just then, she saw a paddle boat coming towards her. 'I have to go now,' she said and hurried to the inside of her home.

I resumed my walk in deep thought. What an interesting morning!

I often waved at Ayesha during my morning walks. Once, I saw her feeding *chotchwor* and chai to a young boy who must be about four. She hurriedly started cleaning his face with her scarf when she saw me. 'He's my son.' Pointing to her husband, who was rowing a paddle boat towards the deep waters, she said, shyly, 'Mushtaq *jaan*.'

I found it quite romantic the way she had added '*jaan*' to her husband's name. She must really love him to call him '*jaan*' or 'life.'

While watching her, I often felt a need to get rid of the chains that bound me. I was reminded when during a school picnic at the Wular lake, I had walked away from the group of children, stepped into a boat and forcefully paddled away from the bank on my own. It was such a liberating moment. I sat there for a while in solitude, not wanting to go back. I even let the paddles go and watched them as they floated away from the boat. The teachers and helpers who had come to the picnic to take care of us were dismayed. I ignored their cries of 'stay still; don't move.' Looking at the faces of the girls gave me a huge satisfaction. My unabashed recklessness! My independence and defiance! How they envied and hated me! What a feeling, to be living on your own, with those who you choose, the ones you proudly announce to the world as your *jaan*, your life.

I had read somewhere that our situation in life, the turn of events, and the highs and lows are the cumulative effect of the various choices we make. Why then, even with the best of my efforts, was I not able to escape my fate? I was just out of school when I told my father that I wanted to be a doctor. I had thought he would be very pleased.

But he had laughed aloud, called his pretty wife over and told her in the most humiliating tone, '*Lo bhai, Doctorsaahiba se milo*, meet the lady doctor.'

She gave me a beatific smile. 'Oh! So, you actually had written her off as a *gupna* doctor, a doctor of cattle?' she said, chiding her husband.

My stepbrothers had been fascinated by the word '*gupna doctor.*' Pulling at my shirt, they kept chanting it, long after I had left the room in tears.

I packed my suitcase the day my result was announced. What would have been a day of joyous celebration in any other household, was like a normal day in my house. There were no celebratory calls from relatives. Nobody arrived with sweets and bakery, nor was I pampered and showered with expensive gifts. My father came to know of my admission to a prestigious medical college in Bombay only when he received a letter, asking him to complete the formalities. Although the classes would start in a couple of months, I insisted on going anyway.

That night, I had overheard my stepmother telling my father to reconsider sending me to Bombay. 'Think of the expenses. Bombay is expensive, especially the hostel,' she had said, to a man who could afford to buy the whole building if he wished.

He had looked at her with loving eyes and sighed. 'At least she will be out of your hair.'

There was much more to medicine than I had bargained for. I remained a below-average student, no matter how much I tried. Survival was tough, but I held on. I sought no friendships, no relationships. I watched as, within a few months of joining, each of my classmates became a part of a group, some small, others rather large. I was always alone, whether in the classroom or the canteen. I had to share my hostel room with a Keralite girl, who did not even bother to introduce herself. Two months later, she was gone, having moved into a single room, on the other end of the floor. The new roommate was a revelation from the word go. I found her sprawled on my side of the room, fast asleep when I returned from my classes one day. I was hovering over the heater which I had managed to sneak into the hostel room. We were not allowed to cook in the rooms, but I reckoned breaking this one law would solve the problem of my perpetual hunger. When I heard a movement behind me, my first instinct was to push the heater under my bed.

With a stinging slap on my back, she uttered her first words to me, '*Bindaas rehne ka*' a line I got used to with time, which meant 'stay cool' in the quintessential *Bombaiya* language.

Nimmi was very average looking, but her mass of thick curly hair, which she styled differently every time she stepped out, gave her a look of a ramp model. She was a year older than me and in no manner did she look like she was on her way to become a doctor. I was quite surprised to learn that she was actually a brilliant student. She would always be found in shorts and the briefest vest I had ever seen. Her hyperactive mind flew in a dozen directions at one time. There was no stopping her chatter. Her voice was hoarse and loud. She could never sit still, even while eating. I was drawn to her like a magnet. Within days of meeting her, I felt lighter and the world seemed a bit kinder.

'*Gokha heran dula, dudye mas*,' she uttered loudly one Valentine's Day while barging in suddenly into our tiny room, shutting the door behind her with a bang.

She had a packet of Dunhill cigarettes wrapped with a ribbon in her hand.

'Wait, what was that?' I could hardly control my laughter.

'It took me a whole day to learn some lines to woo my Kashmiri boyfriend,' she said, plonking herself on her bed.

'And do you know what you are about to tell him?'

'That he is a handsome devil and let's elope!' she said, with a smug smile while running her fingers through a long shiny curl.

'You idiot, it means hope you fall down the stairs and hope your hair catches fire!'

She jumped up and got hold of my hand while running down two steps at a time to the first floor where the senior girls stayed. She demanded that I shout curse words in Kashmiri behind closed doors. 'You are mad,' is all I could say angrily, but she dug her nails into my hand while giving me a murderous look.

'*Peyi thraath*,' I said weakly.

'What does it mean?'

'May lightning strike you.'

She licked her lips with satisfaction and yelled '*PEYI THRAATH*. Give me another one.'

'*Shikasladin,*'

'*SHIKASLADIN,*' she shouted while running out of the building at fast as she could, dragging me behind her, all along telling me how she had stood outside the rooms of the girls who had made a fool of her and taught her curse words instead of the romantic lines that she had wanted to learn in Kashmiri.

Mustahassan greeted her with a hug and winked at me behind her back. Tall, lanky, with light brown hair and a blonde moustache, he looked like someone right out of Debonair.

'*Ek ke saath ek free,*' he joked.

When Nimmi asked what he meant, he kissed the tip of her nose and touched my nose with one finger, 'I mean, I'm lucky to get to date two lovely girls at the same time on Valentine's Day.'

'She's here for me, not you. Just in case I get bored with you,' Nimmi laughed.

They were Nims and Mush to each other. We spent an uneventful evening driving around the busy streets of Worli in Mustahassan's Santro. Loud rock music drowned any conversation. We stopped for ice cream. Nimmi had her arm around Mustahassan's waist, while I stood a foot away. Mustahassan suggested we play a game.

'Let's see who can eat the most ice cream in 10 mins. The winner gets to choose a gift, which the others will have to pay for,' he suggested.

'You just wait! I'll never let a Kashmiri beat me in an ice cream eating competition!' I announced excitedly, grabbing his half-eaten orange bar.

Nimmi's mood changed suddenly. She grew sullen and withdrawn. 'Sara, let's go home. I'm tired,' she said.

'Nims, let's stay for a while. Don't spoil the fun,' Mustahassan said.

I was a little confused and didn't know how to react. She had already hopped into a cab. Her middle finger jutting out of the cab window, taunting us.

'She's probably got a headache,' I said, defending my friend.

'She's crazy,' said her angry boyfriend.

He didn't offer to drop me at the hostel.

I met her a week later at the college canteen.

A tap on the shoulder and a familiar voice said, 'Hey, you stranger.'

'Where have you been?' I inquired.

'None of your business,' she replied, in a teasing tone.

I wanted to leave, but she wouldn't let go of my hand. It made me smile when she broke into an old Hindi song '*Na rootho rootho na rootho na rootho meri jaan.*' Her comical antics made everyone around laugh. They clapped as she sang and danced around me. We went to the hostel together. Nimmi was her normal boisterous self again. There was no explanation for her weird behaviour on Valentine's Day. Although I was dying to ask, something held me back.

She would often disappear for weeks. I assumed she had a study partner to help her revise during exams. Meanwhile, I was clearly struggling. Just making an appearance in the class made me apprehensive and nervous. I tried to make myself as inconspicuous as possible and succeeded to a large extent. But there was no way I could escape the assessments. They were always brutally tough. I often thought of leaving it all and going away. But go where? My father called once in a while, mostly to check if I had received the money that he had transferred to my account. In my two years in Bombay, I hadn't had a single letter or phone call from anyone else, nor was I asked to come home to spend vacations. In any case, I preferred not to go.

'What a waste! You are 20, and you are in Bombay, and all you have tasted is life in a humdrum classroom, or your cubbyhole of a hostel room,' said Sarika, my next-door neighbour, taking a drag from a cigarette, as we lounged around the railing connecting the line of rooms on the second floor of the hostel.

I took in the view below with a fresh perspective. A couple of under-dressed girls were hurrying to their rooms while carrying trays of bland, tasteless dinner. A Manipuri girl, who was in my class, was talking in a loud shrieking voice on the payphone on the ground floor, while a couple of other girls were urging her to hang up. A tall, fair senior was wrapping her freshly washed long brown hair in a towel. "*This has been my life in Bombay,*" I thought.

'You never gave yourself a chance,' said Sarika, who would be a brilliant psychiatrist one day.

Nimmi had been talking about her plans to spend a few days in Mahableshwar. I'd seen the pictures of the lovely place just a few hours' drive away from Bombay. Cool breeze, a walk along the banks of a beautiful lake, quaint little marketplaces selling fresh strawberries, squashes and jams. Just the thought of it made me nostalgic. A rare outing along the Boulevard in Srinagar brushed my memory. I must have been around ten. Daddy had been in a jovial mood that day. He had a meeting to attend in the Nehru Park area and had unexpectedly decided to take me with him. How timid and shy I had been at first, not knowing how to talk to him throughout the way in his car. As he met with his client, I sat outside his office on a large lawn overlooking Dal Lake. It was a bright, sunny afternoon. I watched with envy as tourists haggled with the *shikara* owners, their kids rushing towards the ice cream carts. I was surprised when Daddy decided to take the car towards the Boulevard, instead of home, which was on the opposite side. For the next couple of hours, we were just driving up and down the hairy bends of the Shankracharya Hill at top speed, gaping at the city below from Pari Mahal and watching the sunset at the Nishat Bagh. He had urged me to keep the windows down, to breathe in the fresh, cool air, to look for the colours in the sunset I had never noticed before. When we reached home, while still in the car, I looked at him with a smile, expecting him to smile back at me. But he had just walked towards the house without even glancing at me.

How I wished Nimmi would extend an invitation to me. I decided to drop in a few hints.

'So, it's gonna be a long weekend and I don't even have a book to read,' I said.

There was no answer. I had been complaining about Bombay's hot and humid weather, the mosquitoes, and the boring company of the hostel girls for 10 minutes now and she had remained silent, staring at the ceiling, her hair falling off the back of the chair on which she was sitting, legs on the bed.

Finally, I decided to be direct. 'Can I come with you to Mahableshwar?'

She sat up, gave me a strange smile and said, 'Sure, why not?'

They say, there comes a life-altering turn in everyone's path of life. You just have to be aware of that moment. Whether you take it or not, is a choice you make. I walked that path when I took that trip to Mahableshwar with Nimmi. It would be a new beginning for me. I would finally let go of my past, which had given me nothing but pain and regret. It was time to build new relationships, and chart out a future from a present that would fill my heart with all that I would cherish for a lifetime. It was the single happiest day of my life, standing in the lush green meadows under the gentle sun, letting the sounds and smells of nature soothe my nerves and completely relax and heal me.

Nimmi had been in very good humour throughout the drive to Mahableshwar. I never asked about the car. It looked like she had borrowed it. Together, we sang romantic songs from our childhood. I told her about how I would wait for Sunday afternoon to listen to the

Western music request show on Radio Kashmir, and my first crush who happened to be the guy with the deep voice presenting it. I learnt a few things about her that she never had mentioned before. Like her parent's divorce, her traumatised childhood with a mother who was struggling with mental illness and the lonely years in a strict convent boarding school. Confiding in each other was the cornerstone of a long-lasting friendship, I thought. My convictions were the first ones to be sacrificed on the altar of betrayal.

A bungalow tucked away behind acres of fruit gardens. We reached this enchanted Eden late in the evening. Nimmi unlocked a room on the second floor.

'I'll see you downstairs after you freshen up,' she said with a smile.

I wasn't bothered much about the room, although I felt it had not been cleaned for a while. The windows were closed and it had a strange smell. As I looked outside, I saw Nimmi talking to a tall, pretty girl in a short dress. She looked up and waved at me. I could see a hint of amusement in the girl's eyes. I shrugged off the feeling of discomfort and took a quick wash.

As I walked downstairs, I heard loud voices, talking incessantly. There was a hush as I entered the semi-circular room which had half a dozen French windows. There were four girls, some around my age, some maybe a couple of years older, sitting on a leather sofa. The room was tastefully done, with large paintings, carved furniture and a huge chandelier in the centre.

Nimmi walked towards me with arms outstretched. 'Guys, introducing…,' she began with a flourish, 'What shall we call her?'

'Hi, I'm…,' I said a little nervously.

'*Shhh*…' she kept a finger on my lips. 'Don't break the tradition. Every newcomer is given a nickname. So, guys, don your creative hats.'

I stood there getting conscious of my faded jeans and red shirt, which was also one of my favourites. I noticed the girls in the room wore expensive casual clothes, mostly in very light shades. Loose-fitting T-shirts covered non-existent shorts or skirts. Even their flat sandals screamed the most expensive brands. I felt overdressed. A lot of snacks were lying around on the centre table which had not been touched. Everyone was drinking, although I couldn't be sure if it was alcohol. Around six guys were in the back of the room playing snooker. None of them bothered to look in my direction.

'Laska, let's call her Laska,' said a girl with too many rings on her fingers and heavily kohled eyes. She had a small silver ring on her pierced upper lip. Her dark short cropped hair made her look like someone from a rock band.

Nimmi was the first one to react. 'What, and make her disappear? Don't you remember what happened to the last Laska?' This made a few of them giggle. I didn't get the joke, but I found myself grinning as well.

'White Fang, I think it will suit this PYT.'

'White Fang it is,' they said in chorus.

The boys then joined us. One of them handed me a coke. I had noticed him when I entered the room. He was good-looking, wearing a light blue T-shirt and white shorts. His slight stubble and killer smile made me a little weak in the knees. I headed towards one of the beanbags near a window when the girls started arguing about who I should be sitting next to since I was the guest of honour. Flattered, I went to sit in the middle of the sofa, between the girls.

I had a feeling that they were all suddenly interested in me. I also noticed that none of them had introduced themselves. Nimmi was very excited, almost hyperactive. She came up with a game. Apparently, it was something they had devised among themselves and called it Bumblebee.

'It's no rocket science. Just play along and you will learn,' she said to me.

The girl with short hair said something in the ear of the handsome guy and blindfolded him with a scarf. While the others dispersed, I remained rooted on the sofa. I watched him as he slowly approached and touched my arm. I could feel the most tingling, delicious feeling.

'White Fang, you are our master, and we are your slaves,' he said.

'So, what am I expected to do?'

'You can choose to be anything, except human. How about a dog? You will have to chase us cats away. Also, the one cat you catch will have to do exactly what you demand.'

I got up and said in a fierce voice, 'I, White Fang, command you to go hide.' I even added a few barks for effect.

Thus began a game, or so I thought, which brought out the side of me that had never seen the light of day. I was lively. I was funny. I was adorable. I was smart. I was finally in control. And most of all, I was admired, or even envied at some point. The strategies I devised to make them do my bidding! How they loved it all! After just an hour into Bumblebee, there was an electrifying excitement around. They wouldn't get enough of it. I took up the avatar of a dog, running around barking orders, drinking from a dish, peeing on the leg of the centre table, my tongue hanging out. I jumped on the sofa, nuzzled them, licked their faces. They loved my act. They patted me, told me how they had missed me. After a while, I had got so carried away that I had forgotten that they were supposed to be my slaves; they were supposed to be the cats that I commanded over. But never mind, I was tossed from person to person, patted, given a biscuit and asked to roll over. Nimmi asked me to drink coke from a dish she placed on the floor. I lapped it up with glee.

I heard 'Good girl,' 'My BFF,' 'I want to take you home.' I felt happy to be among people who really liked me.

I woke up with a sore back and a throbbing head. My eyes were unable to focus in the darkness. A little disoriented, I tried to recollect where I was. There was silence all around. I got up and walked unsteadily towards the curtains. Drawing them apart, I looked around the room as it got flooded with light. It was in total disarray, with plates, bottles and cushions scattered all over the floor. But my heart skipped a beat when I noticed that I was alone. I looked out of the window. The previous night there were at least three cars parked there. They were gone. I dragged myself from room to room. I even checked the bathrooms. No one. They had all left.

I kept thinking about Nimmi and her friends on the bus on the way back to Bombay. I should have known. Laska and White Fangs were names of dogs from books I had read long ago. They had deliberately staged this evening purely for their entertainment at my expense. My drink had most probably been spiked with drugs. No wonder, I had felt so excited. I had gone to great lengths to please them, to be one of them. To be accepted, that in itself was such a great high. How stupid of me! How easily I had fallen into a trap! What hurt me most was that it was Nimmi, my only friend, who had orchestrated it. Anger spewed inside my heart ready to burst out like lava from a volcano.

Chapter 3

By the time I reached the hostel, two things were clear to me. I had to convince my dad to hand over my mother's property to me. I had known all along that the house belonged to my mother. She came from a renowned business family and had got a huge dowry with her, which also included a lot of jewellery. I didn't yet know what I would do with it, but I was sure I would learn to invest it in a business of my own. Another thing was that I didn't want to be a doctor anymore.

I reached Srinagar the same evening. I was not ready for such a big change in the house where I had spent my entire childhood. Two huge Alsatian dogs barked at me excitedly as I opened the gate. They looked ferocious, but thankfully, they were tied to a tree on the other end of the lawn. The lawn itself was unkept, with autumn leaves strewn all over. The rose bushes that I had loved were gone and the cherry trees I sat under on warm summer days looked sad and abandoned. The clank of metal from the balcony on the upper floor caught my attention. A heavyset bearded man in a blue tracksuit was lifting weights. A new set of rooms had been constructed on the right corner of the house. Without a glance inside, I walked towards my room. When I opened the door, I was shocked to see that it had a complete makeover. None of the things belonging to me was there. Sleeping on the bed on his stomach was another stranger, a boy wearing a black T-shirt and jeans. He hadn't even bothered to remove his shoes.

'Sarahjaan,' I heard a feeble voice behind me.

I turned around as an old woman walked swiftly towards me. It was difficult to recognise her at first. But the moment she held my head in her hands and showered kisses all over my face, I knew it was Zooni, my stepmother's old faithful. She had come as *dodhmouj* with her dowry. A maid who would be her eyes and ears in the new family, and she had remained so all these years. I wanted to tear away from her sweaty smell and her rotten breath, but she held me close.

'*Balai lagai, rathchep wandai,*' her blessings sounded hollow, and her marble-like wicked blue eyes twinkled.

She caught hold of my hand and took me to the third floor of the house. I could hear the jangling of keys in her turquoise *pheran* pocket. She opened the door to the attic. '*Balai lagai*, we didn't know you were coming. You can stay here now. I'll get it cleaned. *Meya lagi na kihin, sheen hui karay kamara*. I'll clean the room in a jiffy, as pristine as snow,' she said, before leaving me in a 10X6-foot room full of trunks and wooden crates. A tiny dirty window looked over the backyard, where I saw Zooni fill my stepmother with details of my homecoming.

She was sitting on a hammock, probably drying her long hair in the sun. A book lay on her lap. She glanced up at me and went back to her book. I asked Zooni about my father when she came back huffing and puffing with a broom and a mop.

'*Haay. Kya wanai. Haejsaab chu bisstaras larith gomut. Tamis bechaaras chu na kihin roodmut.* Haajisaab is bedridden and very weak.'

Alarmed, I ran down the stairs to my father's room. No one had told me about my father's illness. I was fuming. As I knocked on his door, there was no reply. I peeped in and saw him sitting on a chair by the window with a heavy blanket on his knees. His head was almost bald, his cheeks hollow. As he turned towards me, I was horrified to see his sunken lifeless eyes. He looked away as soon as he saw me. There were no words to welcome me.

'Why are you here, have you run away from college?' he said angrily. '*Kyha goi! Kuas laanat asek zaamech tamis maaji*,' spiteful words, cursing me and my mother.

'I have come back to take what is mine,' I said, hating the sound of my voice.

I hadn't noticed that my stepmother had crept in behind me. '*Acchaa*,' she said with her hands on her hips. 'What is this new thing I'm hearing?'

'I'm talking about my mother's property and jewellery.' She looked most amused as she walked towards my father. 'Let me help you, you must be tired. Go to bed,' she said softly. My father obeyed her as if he was hypnotised. He slowly got up and lay down on his bed. She stood there against the window, her long wet hair shimmering. Her midnight blue silk *kaftan* fell loosely over her slim waist, making her look like an exotic bird. 'Go back, complete your education. After that, we will see,' she said.

'I'm not going back. From now on, I will be living here in my mother's house,' I shouted, seething with anger.

'Who has filled your head with garbage? This house belongs to me. My husband has handed it over to me. As for your mother's jewellery, this is the first time I'm hearing anything about it.' I'd hoped my father would be supportive. But he remained silent, with closed eyes, not listening to a single word I had said.

Days turned into a month. My father had not spoken to me again.

'Daddy,' I had asked him, 'Why did you keep me in the care of nannies when I could have been with you?'

That was one time when he had looked directly at me, and said with much conviction, 'Every time I saw your face, I was reminded of how your mother died. I loved her a lot. The doctors had told her not to conceive after she had a miscarriage, but she was adamant. She died of complications she got during your birth.'

He had passed away a few days later. I felt like a hollow shell, with my insides taken away and buried with him. The month that followed was of fervent activity. There were many ceremonies organised for the departed soul. Dozens of people, mostly my stepmother's relatives and friends came to offer their condolences. She sat quietly every day in the corner of the tent erected on the front lawn, looking dazzling in her dark *salwar kameez*, head covered. The *waza* was kept busy serving at least 20 people every day, and on the fortieth day, there was a grand dinner. I watched as the guests wolfed down the scrumptious meal as if it was their last.

My stepmother's two brothers were now permanent fixtures in the house. The elder one, Amir, the burly bearded one, never talked to me. He would leave the house, invariably after having a heavy breakfast of roast chicken or mutton *kababs* with a couple of heavily buttered *tandoori rotis,* always returning late at night. Basit, who was around 26, must be younger to his brother by about three years. I would see him mostly loitering around the house, sleeping till late afternoon and doing mostly nothing. He was his sister's driver and right-hand man. They lived a life of luxury, wearing expensive clothes and watches, and having a feast every night. I could hear laughter till early morning from my father's room. I felt jealous to the core.

I broached the subject of my inheritance once again with my stepmother. It was a cold winter morning. It had snowed that night, the first snow of the season. As I entered the kitchen, I saw her sitting with her brothers with a spread of steaming *harissa* on the *dastarkhwan*.

'Come, Amir has got this *harissa* from a famous shop in Batmaloo. It's the best place for *harissa*.'

She was in good humour. She even served me a *kabab* and asked Zooni to heat up the *rotis* for me.

'Wait, you need to serve it by pouring hot oil on it.'

She clapped her hands like a child as Zooni poured hot mustard oil over my plate of *harissa*.

'Hear that sizzle? That's what I love about *harissa*,' she giggled.

Amir and Basit too were smiling. I lingered on after the heavy breakfast, as *nun chai* was being made in a samovar for this special occasion of '*sheen mubarak*,' or 'first snow.'

'I need to know if you have my father's will.' I decided to be blunt.

She seemed to be waiting for this, as she did not show any emotions; no surprise, no anger.

'It is true. This house and the 5-acre land it stands on has been left to you,' she said. 'But it comes with a rider. The papers will be handed to you on the day of your marriage.'

I was flabbergasted.

'Your father has mentioned it in his will,' she said in a steely voice. 'I can show you the papers. In fact, Fawaadsaahib, the lawyer, will visit us today and you can talk to him and clear all your doubts. As for the jewellery you claim to be your mother's, let me tell you that there is no such thing. But I have kept some pieces for your marriage. The least I can do for a motherless girl.'

I was in a daze for days. It looked like she was right. Fawaadsaahib, who was an affectionate, fatherly figure, suggested that I get married at the earliest.

'*Beta*, be careful about who you choose, *baaki Allah ki marzi*,' he said, removing his *karakuli* cap with one hand and giving his head a vigorous scratch with the other.

The excitement of finding a groom for me grew in the household from that day. Zooni was kinder to me. She would bring me hot tea and biscuits in the cold mornings and a hot water bottle at night. My stepmother would spend hours discussing my trousseau. She knew about all the good tailors and fabric showrooms in Srinagar. Her knowledge of fashion astonished me. A *manzimour* – a professional matchmaker – started making rounds of the house. His heavily kohled eyes and bejewelled fingers reminded me of the *nautch* girls in old historical Hindi films. Every prospective match, according to him, was perfect for me. All of them were rich and handsome with wonderful, loving families dying to welcome me to their homes. It was my stepmother who would find some fault in each of them.

'This one here looks like a crook.' 'I know this one's mother. She'll eat my little girl alive,' '*kaacha tyambar cheye*,' she abused him. 'This one is gay. How dare you seek an alliance with him!'

Then, one day, she showed me a photograph of someone I knew. It was of my college friend Shazia's brother, Parvez. I remembered him as a show-off, spoilt, rich guy. He most certainly had many girlfriends. I was surprised that he was still single. That night, I called up Shazia. She seemed thrilled and repeated the words she had said a long time ago when we studied together. 'Parvezbhaijan is a wonderful, generous guy and my mother is the most caring person. You will have a great family, full of love and support.' I had no reason to say no to Parvez.

My *nikah* ceremony was during a lovely spring afternoon. My groom would come with the *baraat* in the evening and take me with him to my new universe. I was exhausted. I was about to lock the door of my room, hoping to get some rest, when my stepmother entered with her two brothers. She got hold of my hand and made me sit on the bed.

Towering over me, with her brothers looking over her shoulders, she hissed, 'Sign these papers.'

I looked at her in confusion.

'Sign the papers,' she repeated.

I tried to read the legal document she had thrust into my hands, but my tears blinded my eyes.

'No crying,' she was wagging her finger in front of my face. 'You are gifting all your share of the property to me. So, sign it.'

I was trembling now. She held my shoulders so tightly, they hurt. She then cupped my chin in her hand and with her face inches away from mine, hissed, 'Sign it or you will have to sign your divorce papers. The choice is yours.'

I saw my future crumbling before me with every passing day. Parvez did not show an iota of interest in me. I should have known, even after our engagement, he had not tried to contact me once. He was demanding, abusive and ill-tempered. If he wasn't at the golf course, he was most certainly at an elite club, playing snooker and drinking with his friends. He lived with his mother, who with her shrill voice and dominating presence, would yell at the servant Kaka all the time. She was obese and short and wore tight satin suits with oversized sweaters. She was always sweating, even when it was cold. Kaka would dutifully hand her a large box of medicines after every meal, and she would gulp down dozens of tablets at a time, always complaining, always sulking.

'*Mey aasa kam bemari nata*, Didn't I have enough diseases….' she would say looking at me with poison in her eyes.

I pretended to not understand at all. I heard when she called me a 'disease' or 'ungrateful,' or 'useless,' or a 'leech.' But with time, I learnt not to understand at all.

Chapter 4

I first met Ayesha after about ten years of living as Parvez's wife. The unusual friendship with the fisherwoman brought back some normalcy and a glimmer of hope in my listless life. I would especially take the route of the Boulevard, where she usually stationed her little boathouse. Every day, I would learn something new about her simple life as the wife of a fisherman, a nomad with no attachment to the land or the people on it. I would sometimes get gifts for her son, Dilawar. A toy motor boat, a Pokemon T-shirt or imported chocolate bars. He was especially thrilled with the handheld Pacman game I got for him.

I would think of Ayesha throughout the day after coming back from my walk. I would daydream of living on a boat, away from the rest of the world. In my imagination, my boat would be moored far away, all alone in the centre of the lake, maybe a bigger lake, where no one could see me. An idea started to grow in my mind. With each passing moment, it grew bigger and bigger. It was completely undoable and bizarre, but I could not shake it off. Like Jack's magic beanstalk, my belief touched the sky. I would snatch from life what was rightfully mine, the luxury of doing what I wanted, to go where I pleased, to love who I wanted. My fate lines were waiting for a knife to change their course. I would not hold back this time. I would carve them myself, even if I bled to death in the process. I spent days convincing myself that I was not doing anything wrong. That it was the only way for me. That I was not doing any injustice to Ayesha, only doing her a favour. I would free Ayesha of her sorry existence and give her a fresh lease of life. And I would take her place, as her fisherman husband Mushtaq's new wife.

After innumerable attempts at giving a direction to my plan, I hit upon an idea.

'Aren't you worried about the militancy here?' I asked Ayesha when I met her next.

'*Humko kya karenge*? Why would they trouble us?' she replied in all innocence.

'You know how they hate non-Kashmiris,' I lied.

But this didn't seem to bother her. Over the next few meetings, I would fill her with many kinds of lies, like how a woman was kidnapped just because she was an outsider, how an entire family was burnt alive in a fire because the militants suspected they had a love marriage, how a man was forced to divorce his wife of many years because she was a non-Muslim. Ayesha began to show some signs of distress after a while. She would hold her son close and whisper sweet endearments as if she was deeply afraid that he would be snatched away. Her husband, Mushtaq, once came over to talk to me. I noticed his skin was rugged and suntanned, but he was handsome too. He asked me if it was true that their lives were in danger.

'Yes, I care for your wife and son, that's why I'm telling you this.'

Mushtaq and Ayesha were getting worried. But for my plan to succeed, I needed her to leave him. What if he decides to move the family elsewhere? I had to act fast. To my amazement, the person who I least expected came to my rescue. My stepmother's brother, Amir. I had learnt that he had turned into a hardcore militant. One Sunday afternoon, he and a few of his fellow militants had sneaked into our house and taken refuge in one of the rooms. Parvez had strictly instructed my mother-in-law and me from entering the room in which they were hiding. I got a chance to talk to him when he was leaving. I called him Amir *Maamu*, which seemed to please him.

'Can you help me?' I pleaded.

He rested his right hand on his chest and said, 'Of course.' He then gave me his phone number and asked me to call him.

Amir was quick and efficient. After all, he wanted to prove to me that he was not the good-for-nothing that I had once called him on his face. He kidnapped Mushtaq. This gave me ample opportunity to brainwash Ayesha. At first, she was inconsolable. She wanted to go to the police. But I told her they would kill her instead.

'Think of your son. The police would rather get rid of you, than look for your husband. It would be easier for them.' I promised her I would talk to my husband, and together, we would find a way to rescue him. Meanwhile, she and her son would have to leave. 'Go back to your village. I'll arrange for your air tickets. I'll come tomorrow with the tickets. Leave this place, and save your lives,' I told her in my best reassuring voice.

I had looked forward to this dawn for so long. I had Ayesha's and her son's air tickets to Patna in my pocket. I had waited for nearly two hours on the banks of Dal Lake, waiting for a glimpse of her boat. But this was the first time that she didn't turn up for our daily rendezvous. By evening, I was a bundle of nerves. I sat on the cold cement steps outside my house for a long time that night, sad and distraught. Around midnight, my phone rang. It was Ayesha. She explained that her son had hurt his hand while playing.

'*Palastar karna pada*,' she explained. I was too excited to hear the rest of her story.

'Be ready at 7 tomorrow morning. I'll take you to the airport,' I said.

Amir had played his role well. He had put so much fear in Mushtaq that he promised not to take Ayesha's name ever again. I started my early morning walks again on the Boulevard. With time, it was Mushtaq who had replaced Ayesha as my companion for a few stolen moments.

My life has a new name – *Jaan*. As I sit on a wooden box inside this tiny smelly boat, I can see the shimmering water on the horizon welcoming me to my new home.

THE END

STEEL

PART 1

There couldn't have been a more radiant bride. Full of dignity and pride, she surveyed the room, her green and gold *sharara* complementing her flashing eyes of the same colour. She was covered in heavy jewellery, literally from head to toe. Her mother sat next to her, quiet and still. More like a marble statue, expressionless. The bride, not yet twelve, was sitting on the *masnand*, a silk carpet especially laid out for her, with such grace that the mother felt her chest swell with pride. She surveyed the tastefully decorated tent where dozens of ladies had gathered.

Raising her hand, she startled them when she said in a loud voice, 'Where is the *wanwun*, the wedding songs? Why is everyone huddled in corners?'

A few women gathered, and holding each other by the shoulder, surrounded the bride while attempting a feeble song. The bride's mother got up to her full height and stood right in the centre. In a booming voice that could be heard in the neighbouring tent, where the men were having their dinner, she sang, '*Shubdaar Maharaniye*, my most beautiful bride,' urging the women to join her. None of them could ignore her magnetic presence. Soon, there were two groups of women standing in front of the bemused bride, singing in chorus and dancing to the *wanwun*, wishing her a wonderful married life, telling her how beautiful she looked and how lucky the bridegroom was to have her as his bride.

'*Wachiy amis kun, ye Bilquis hai cha zan kain*, look at Bilquis, she seems to be made of stone,' gossiped the women about the mother of the bride.

'*Aush katara chus na achen manz. Kus waniy jawaan kur trawen raath hi kabari manz*, not a tear in her eyes. Who will believe that she buried her young daughter just yesterday!'

Bilquis knew that she was under the scrutiny of many eyes, all waiting to pounce on her the moment she showed a moment of weakness. But she was determined, as she adjusted the diamond-encrusted *kasaaba* – a traditional headgear – on her daughter's head, that she would never give them that satisfaction.

'*Yem lavnai na chaiyenis pozaaras*, they are not even worth your footwear,' she whispered in the ear of her beloved daughter.

Sardara took it all in as if preparing for war. She may have had marriage thrust upon her unexpectedly, but she most certainly was not her sister. "*Maheen had been a meek mouse from the beginning*," she thought. Although she was elder to Sardara by six years, she had, for some reason, been the one afraid of her younger sister.

Dastarkhawn was being laid for the ceremonial dinner. The bride was the first one to be served. A *trami*, a large copper plate meant to serve four, laden with a whole roast chicken, four pieces each of *tabak maaz* and *kabab* were piled on a huge mound of rice. As was the tradition, the bride, the groom's mother and her two daughters would be eating from the same *trami*.

But as they got up to join her, Sardara said in a very clear voice, '*Mai naz chuna aadat kainsi si seet khyun trami manz*, I don't have a habit of sharing my *trami* with anyone.'

A hushed silence followed as her mother-in-law stopped in her tracks. The story was told and retold many times, and the child bride became a legend overnight.

Bilquis was not surprised by Sardara's behaviour. Unlike Maheen, she had always had a mind of her own. Munnawar, her husband, had often pointed out, asking her to discourage Sardara from being so insensitive and rude.

'Her behaviour will be her ruin,' he had warned Bilquis.

'Oh, she would rather be a meek spectator, a worm to be trampled upon, like some of us,' Bilquis thundered.

Munnawar knew she was referring to their elder daughter Maheen and him in particular. The owner of one of the biggest carpet businesses in Kashmir in the 50s, who presided over a staff of nearly 300 and had a turnover that went into crores, held his head in his hands, closed his eyes and let the wave of shame pass.

Sardara had got her obstinate and temperamental streak from her mother, something that Munnawar understood very well. He had first got a glimpse of this side of his wife's nature on the day he married her. He already had a wife, Safiya, lovingly called Safilala, a quiet, pious soul who had devoted her life to looking after his huge house and every comfort. She, however, hadn't been able to fulfil his deepest desire – to give him a son. A couple of miscarriages later, he had completely given up. Safilala had profusely apologised and begged for another chance, but by then, his friend Jaleel had subtly hinted about his sister Bilquis.

'Not only will she give you sons, but you will also never tire of her beauty,' he had said temptingly.

Jaleel had earlier missed the opportunity of getting his sister married to the fabulously rich Munnawar, who also came from one of the most respected families in Srinagar. This time, he would grab the opportunity with both hands. This was one chance for redemption for Jaleel's clan. His mother had a dubious background, which was still being gossiped about behind his back. Although his father was from a respectable upper caste family, he had married Zeenat Begum, who some said, was a *nautch* girl. Although the couple had moved out and cut all connections with her family, the stigma was not easy to erase.

'You don't have to divorce Safilala. They will both live happily together,' Jaleel had said, setting the bait.

He had then invited his friend to a ten-course *wazwaan* dinner at his house where he was introduced to Bilquis. One look at her and Munnawar was floored. Her skin was as if it had been dipped in milk, long lashes fanned her big green eyes, while golden tresses fell over her voluptuous hips. After a sleepless night, Munnawar had sent a marriage proposal to her. Within a week, the *nikah* ceremony was scheduled.

Bilquis watched carefully as the *Qazi* completed the formalities. Just as the handful of guests invited for the *nikah* were getting ready to eat, she summoned the groom to her room, where she told him in no uncertain terms that he would have to get rid of his first wife immediately.

Flabbergasted, he pleaded, his voice quivering, 'But I thought Jaleel has discussed with you that we will all live under the same roof. We have been married for eight years now. She has no clue about my *nikah*. How can I ask her to leave?' His knees buckled as he saw her terrifying anger unfold. Who would have thought that a mere girl would command such a presence? Spitting fire, this angel from heaven had given him orders to get rid of her, or he would lose both his wives.

Munnawar visited Bilquis every day for the next month, trying to coax her to come to his house. He would get her expensive jewellery, which she refused to wear. The trays of exotic sweets he procured from abroad were left outside her room to decay. She did not even bother to glance at the yards of *zarbabth* and velvet fabric he bought for her, especially from China. There came a time when she handed him a legal document asking for a divorce. That proved to be the last day for Safilala in Munnawar's house. He could not bring himself to tell her the truth. However, when he asked her to pack all her clothes and jewellery and move to her widowed mother's place, her sixth sense told her that this would be a permanent arrangement. She had seen changes in her husband's behaviour in the past few weeks. He had remained aloof and tense. He had avoided talking to her and moved into the guest bedroom, citing headache and fatigue. No matter how much she tried to talk to him, he just skirted any conversation with her. As she was leaving, she looked back to have one last look at the home that she had made with so much love.

'Munnawarsaab, *mye haz karzi maaf,* please forgive me,' were her departing words to her husband who could not meet her searching eyes.

Bilquis was just twenty when she took over the reins of Munnawar's household. It was a three-storied building in the Gav Kadal area of Srinagar, where most of the elite class, the traders and businessmen had built lavish homes and showrooms. Within a week, she had replaced the staff: the maids, gardeners and those running random errands. She had personally chosen a handful from the dozens Jaleel had sent to her. They would have to work with her in close quarters. So, she demanded their loyalty to the core. She hated gossip mongers and those who showed any signs of laziness or procrastination. The kitchen fire was lit at the first call of the rooster, where cauldrons of fragrant rice, Munnawar's favourite mutton and green *haakh*, a leafy vegetable he especially relished, were cooked by an experienced old couple who had earlier worked with a *waza*, a professional cook. Nothing escaped her vigilant eyes. If the *rogan josh* did not look the brilliant red of her liking, she would order them to throw it away and start afresh. The *rotis* and *lavasas* brought from the local *tandoor* for breakfast had to be piping hot, and the *tchaman*, cottage cheese, soft and fresh. She changed three milkmen before she settled for the one who sold milk which agreed with her standards. In the backyard, there was a huge *kanz*, a bowl-shaped grinder made of stone, that was used to crush spices. Two of the servants were busy most mornings toiling over it for hours to get freshly ground chillies and condiments to be used in the kitchen. Although most days it was just Munnawar and her who were present at the *dastarkhwan* to have their meals, the feast was enough to feed a dozen people.

She was the complete opposite of Safilala, Munnawar's first wife, who cared deeply for the welfare of the domestic help and their families. They often depended on her help during a crisis, for any health emergency or for wedding expenses. Sometimes, going against the wishes of her husband, she had visited their far-flung families during their hour of need. They were, however, terrified of the new Bibiji. Even the smallest mistake was not pardoned and would most certainly mean a salary cut. Every room in the house, including the large hall on the third floor which was only used on rare occasions, had to be mopped and dusted daily. Linen and curtains were hand-washed regularly, no matter what the weather was like. Carpets that stretched from the outer verandah on the ground floor to the lobby on the third floor had to be scrubbed. She supervised everything herself, ticking off the servants as she went around the house, running her fingers over window panes and railings on the long winding staircases.

'Munnawarsaab,' she had asked once in a husky voice after a hearty meal. 'What if I start going to the office?'

Her husband had looked at her, shocked. 'But, what would you do there? What's the need?' he asked in a feeble voice since his instinct told him that she had already made up her mind.

Eyebrows raised, she just sat there watching him.

'Besides, only men work there, you would be uncomfortable with so many of them around,' he stammered.

'Why should I be uncomfortable? I'll just be there to keep an eye on things. I'm not bothered about any men around me. Remember this, Munnawarsaab. One day, you will thank me.'

She was soon making the rounds of the four-storied office building, which had a huge showroom on the ground floor and a warehouse on the top. At first, she just would sit in any random chair for hours, just watching.

For the dozen men working there, she was fascinating, an enigma. This was the boss's wife. So, no one dared talk to her directly. After a customary *salaam*, they would hurriedly go to their desks and avoid any eye contact with her. Munnawar tried his best to dissuade her from continuing to visit the office.

'It's embarrassing for the others,' he would plead, to which she would just raise the arch of her right eyebrow and say, 'I don't care about anyone's comfort or embarrassment; do you?'

For Munnawar, this was just an introduction to his wife's stubbornness and resolve. He would know with time that once she put her mind to something, it was useless to object or argue. There was a sea change in the ways things were handled at home. The servants seemed more disciplined. The furniture and upholstery that she had completely replaced was more extravagant. The food cooked in his kitchen had a diverse menu. But he missed the chatter in the house when he returned from work earlier, when Safiya was around. The simplicity of his surroundings would comfort him. At dinnertime, when the family and servants shared the meals together, he had felt blessed. Bilquis' meddling would ruin the solace he drew from his work, he feared. Maybe, this was just a passing whim. She was just a matriculate. "*She would soon get too overwhelmed with such a huge setup and give up,*" he had thought.

How wrong he was! Bilquis had a drive that he hadn't seen in anyone else. She would go through old files and study account details like invoices and bills immaculately. The turbaned accountant, Kaulji, was summoned. He watched with amusement as she questioned him incessantly about each and every entry. Mohanlal Kaul was an elderly Kashmiri Pandit, who had served the House of Paradise for two generations having been handpicked by Munnawar's father, late Ameer Sadiq, as his personal assistant when he was just 18. He had seen the phenomenal rise of a tiny store selling cheap trinkets in downtown Nawa Kadal, ambitiously called House of Paradise, to a chain of grand showrooms with silk and woollen hand-woven carpets so magnificent that they were displayed even in royal households abroad. He had been fascinated when he learnt that some of the Memsaabs, the European ladies who visited the showrooms, actually ran their own businesses. Of course, he had met an occasional lady doctor, teacher and even lawyer in Kashmir, but business was a purely male-dominated world. So, when Munnawarsaab introduced him to his wife and told him to teach her the ropes, Kaulji was sure it was just a passing fancy of hers.

In fact, later in the afternoon, when he got a minute alone with his boss, Munnawarsaab whispered to him, '*Ha amis gov manzi shokh office yinuk*, her decision to come to the office was purely whimsical.' He added rather sarcastically, '*Amis cha khabar itkhkyan gara cha chalawan, ithay kyan chalaawi office*, she thinks running an office is as easy as doing housework.'

However, Bilquis wasn't the one to give up so easily. Even pregnancy could not put brakes on her determination. Within two years of joining work, she knew every little detail of Munnawar's huge carpet business like the back of her hand. Even he had to admit that she had become an asset. Her charm and good looks were enough to rope in more customers. He didn't need a PR team to advertise. She singlehandedly took care of that, keeping in touch with important customers, inviting them to exhibitions, sending them cards and gifts on special occasions and sometimes, even throwing lavish parties for them.

There were subtle changes at first, but after a couple of years, Munnawar, as well as the stoic Mohanlal Kaul, noticed the sizable profits as demand for their carpets climbed further. Their respect for Bilquis grew, as she returned to work after just a month of giving birth. Maheen, her firstborn, was weak and sickly. If there was any disappointment of not having borne a boy, Bilquis didn't show it. Munnawar, on the other hand, was thrilled to have a child of his own. He used to call her his moon, his sun, his universe.

'You are the answer to my countless prayers,' he would whisper in her ears.

Though Maheen saw very little of her mother, she did not miss her. On the contrary, she was rather terrified of her mother's overwhelming presence. Bilquis was quick to hire a *dodhmoj*, who would breastfeed the baby. Maheen had been frail and timid from the start. She would easily get startled and she had a piercing cry which would irritate her mother. Her *dodhmoj*, Zanna, a middle-aged woman who had just given birth to her sixth child, was the one who eventually would be responsible for raising Maheen. She left her own children in the care of her mother-in-law and came to live in Paradise Manzil.

The scandalised servants would talk among themselves. '*Zan chan mangta ain mach*, her mother is treating her as if she has been adopted.'

The memories of taunts, the backbiting, and the contemptuous looks that Bilquis and her brother Jaleel got from their father's family were all but forgotten.

'*Muaj chak gaen*, their mother is a prostitute,' their aunts would say.

They had never met any relatives from their mother's side as children, but they were sure she was not a prostitute. Maybe, a dancer from one of the infamous brothels in downtown Srinagar. However, Bilquis was determined to remove that blot from the history of her family. She took great pride in hosting her brother and his family at her bungalow. No stone was left unturned in entertaining them with lavish feasts and expensive gifts. It was important for them to look *khandaani*, a label reserved only for those coming from respectable backgrounds. The two of them soon realised it was easy to buy it with money.

Munnawar's hold on his company soon weakened. Bilquis had made sure that Jaleel's investment, especially since they had started to export, did not go unnoticed. Munnawar often wondered how Jaleel managed to come up with the sizable capital of Rs. 2 crores in such a short time. He had no choice but to make him a partner. By the time Sardara, Munnawar and Bilquis' second daughter arrived, the multi-million-dollar business was practically run by Bilquis and Jaleel, while Munnawar slowly started to take a back seat. He quietly saw his hard work, his sweat and blood, his House of Paradise slipping out of his fingers like fine sand.

However, the pleasure he got out of watching Maheen blossom was unmatchable. She was the balm his troubled heart needed so badly. Her large innocent eyes, shy smile and warm hugs melted his heart. Bilquis had washed her hands off her elder daughter. If it wasn't for her father's constant attention, she would have been like a piece of neglected furniture, stored away in some corner of Paradise Manzil. Munnawar saw himself in his precious daughter. He was afraid that unless she developed a spine of steel, she would end up like him, destitute and powerless.

Bilquis finally did, however, find her match in her second daughter, Sardara. Even as a little girl, she was fiercely independent. She would not be denied anything she pleased. A bewitching beauty, her huge green eyes and golden hair added to her reputation as a firebrand. '*Wezmal*, lightning,' was how she was described by those unfortunate enough to fall prey to her wrath. Her demands grew with time, with the servants and even her elder sister at her beck and call. Six-year-old Maheen had been thrilled to have a sister to play with. Abujaan, her father, would bring the baby to Maheen's room whenever Bilquis needed rest. The two of them soon realised that baby Sardara did not like to be disturbed at all. When they tried to cuddle her, she would scream as if she was being attacked. The beautiful baby never smiled or asked to be picked up. She seemed to be content with just her own company, as long as she was fed and made comfortable. Bilquis, who had always disliked Maheen's timid and shy behaviour, was happy that her younger daughter had taken after her.

Sardara was four when she tried to get rid of her elder sister. She had crept into Maheen's room and tried to smother her with a pillow while she was sleeping. She sat on the pillow while her sister struggled to breathe. It was not long before she dislodged the determined Sardara, but Maheen would never forget the look in her eyes. Sardara was shivering as she fought the nauseous waves of hatred, spite and jealousy.

'It was a mistake, wasn't it?' the elder sister asked with concern as well as trepidation.

'*Dafa kyaz chak na gasan* why don't you get lost!' came her icy reply.

Sardara was waiting for the day her sister would go to a place where no one could ever find her. Maheen never talked about the incident to anyone. There were times when she wished she was bold and confident like Sardara. But an unknown fear had taken root in her. Although her father's presence comforted her, she would have bouts of panic and had started to stammer. No matter how much he questioned her about her anxiety, he never got a proper reply. She would end up embracing him and weeping softly without uttering a word. Sardara never did seek anyone else's company, but she did not grow up to be a loner either. Far from that. She could twist anyone around her little finger with her sweet tongue, or anger tantrums. She was sharp and intelligent, and would never have 'No' for an answer. When she was old enough to go shopping, she would always handpick her own clothes, shoes and toys. She demanded her own personal room when she was six. The food was cooked keeping her preference in mind. She was extremely choosy when it came to the people working in the house. She got a servant fired for talking loudly. She complained to her mother about how she could not stand 'ugly' people and yet another one had to be shown the door. She was hard to please and kept everyone on tenterhooks. Her mother took pride in her, always encouraging her. Her father was, however, rather wary of her.

Munnawar, who was now spending most of his time at home, kept a vigil on his younger daughter. He sensed that Maheen needed to be shielded from Sardara. The two of them were being home tutored by a British lady, Ms. Anne.

Whenever he enquired about their progress from her, she would be all praise for Sardara. 'She is curious, smart with numbers and extremely intelligent.' Her face would, however, fall when she talked about Maheen, 'We are trying. She needs help, but hopefully, will catch up soon.'

He didn't need her to spell out to him that Maheen was least interested in studies. Bilquis, in any case, was never in favour of Maheen taking lessons from Ms. Anne.

'Let her learn to run a household,' she would say to her husband.

Bilquis had assigned Jaleel with a crucial task – that of finding a match for Maheen from one of the wealthiest and the most influential families in Kashmir. She had already made inroads into the higher echelons of the society by marrying Munnawar, but the top one per cent, the super-rich who everyone watched with envy from afar, was still out of her reach. But not for long; Maheen would be the one to lead the way. Jaleel convinced Bilquis to marry her daughter to an epileptic man, senior to Maheen by 15 years. They did not look beyond his palatial house in posh Nigeen and the fact that he was a sole heir of a business tycoon. Munnawar tried to protest. He had, like everyone else in Kashmir, known about the Shah boy who was in and out of hospitals most of his life.

'Would her own uncle harm her in any way?' Bilquis protested. 'Ashraf is totally cured. Yes, he used to have some fits in his childhood, but they can afford the best doctors in the world, can't they? People just want to spread rumours about him. In fact, it was he who first showed interest in our Maheen. He must have seen our beautiful daughter at Raziya's wedding,' she lied.

Munnawar knew it was important to mentally prepare Maheen for the wedding. She grew pale when he broke the news.

'No, no, how can you send me somewhere else? I won't go, Abujaan,' she cried bitterly.

Bilquis had hugged and kissed her. 'You silly girl! I'm sure you must be secretly happy,' she had pinched her, giggling and laughing.

She had already started making elaborate plans for the wedding functions. Jaleel had acted as the middleman between the two families.

'They will be happy if you send her with just a couple of dresses,' he said, singing paeans of the Shah family's fortune.

But Bilquis wanted this to be one wedding that everyone would remember for years. Sardara showed interest in the wedding only when her mother opened the large safe in her bedroom. She had already gone through every piece of jewellery her mother owned.

'There is no need to give her the *kadas* that Abujaan gave you at your wedding, Ami,' she told her mother. 'They are antique pieces. She wouldn't know their value. Buy new jewellery for her.'

As for Maheen, these things never mattered. She was confined to her room ever since she heard about her wedding. The days ahead looked gloomy to her, as if a sword was hanging on her head. Her nervousness grew each day. No one noticed the involuntary twitch of a shoulder whenever the subject of the wedding was brought up in her presence.

Once the alliance was formalised, Ashraf Shah was in a hurry to marry. His mother had been looking for a bride for him for a long time. But his health condition was known to every family in Kashmir, thanks to the thriving grapevine of rumour mongers. Even his own maternal aunt refused to marry her daughter to him. It was heart breaking. So, when Maheen's family approached his mother, she agreed instantly. Disregarding any protests Munnawar would have, the wedding ceremonies were planned within two weeks of the match being fixed. Bilquis took up the herculean task of arranging for the bride's trousseau and the gifts for the groom and his family. All the functions at the bride's house, the *mal manz*, *manz raat* and *yen wol* would be attended by hundreds of guests. Bilquis had refused to invite anyone from her side of the family, except Jaleel and his family.

Elaborate tents were laid out on the sprawling lawns of Paradise Manzil. The *wazas* were instructed to spare no cost. A full 25-course *wazwaan* would be served for all the functions. Famed musicians, who would enthral the guests with *naat sharif* and wedding songs, arrived and took their place in a corner in the central tent. Gifts of silver bangles, silk suits and perfumes were distributed among the women who had come for the *mal manz* ceremony, when the bride's hair was oiled and her body was smeared with aromatic sandalwood paste. Deep inside, Maheen was in turmoil. Marriage scared her. She had not yet learnt to take charge of her own life; how would she manage to live as someone's wife, she wondered. Her anxiety did not let her eat or sleep. She felt sick in the stomach.

'All girls feel like this at the time of marriage. It's the excitement. You are 18; it's time you had a husband and a family of your own,' her mother had told her.

Sardara, who had always been intrigued by the bond her father and sister shared, was happy at the turn of events. So, now her meek sister would leave forever. Sardara never could put a finger on why Abujaan liked her so much. He used to stand between the two sisters like a wall whenever Maheen felt threatened. He did not let her toughen up. He should have let her fight her own battles. The satisfaction would have been different if only the *gagur*, mouse, as she used to call her elder sister, would have stood up for herself. Now that she was leaving, Sardara's interest moved from her sister to her father. Abujaan was biased. He loved Maheen more. But Sardara wanted to make sure that all that would soon change.

Maheen felt dizzy with the weight of the heavy blue velvet *pheran* covered with exquisite silver *tilla* embroidery in the front and sleeves which was especially chosen for her *mehendi* by Ashraf, her groom. She was surprised as Sardara took her hand and started a floral design with henna on it. Maheen held her breath; she wasn't sure what her sister was up to. Sardara made beautiful motifs of lotus flowers on her palms, while grape vines entwined her long fingers. She gave Sardara a shy smile. Just then, Sardara opened her own palms to show her henna. In the centre was a heart shape. Written in Urdu inside was Ashraf + Sardara. Maheen froze, while Sardara laughed aloud.

Paradise Manzil came alive with the buzz of the activities. Bilquis dazzled, smiling at her guests, making sure the important ones got special care. The groom was welcomed with garlands made of roses, cardamoms and currency notes. The guests who arrived with the groom were given a gold coin each, while the groom was lavished with expensive watches, gold chains and rings. When the time to leave arrived, Maheen grew so pale that her father was afraid that she would faint. It was then that Bilquis decided to go with her.

'I'll just make sure that she is comfortable and return,' she told her husband while making the unusual request.

Bilquis had intended to stay in Maheen's new home for just a few hours, but fate had something else planned for her. The ceremony of the reception of the bride ended at midnight. When Ashraf's cousin sisters came to take her to his room, she wouldn't let go of her mother's hand. Bilquis tactfully explained to them that she was not well.

'Let me take care of her tonight. She has had a long day,' she explained adding, '*shur cha, thache mech aise*, she's just a child. She must be tired.' The embarrassed mother scolded Maheen when they were alone in a guest bedroom. 'How long will it take for you to understand? Why do you have to be such a wimp? Any girl would give her right arm to get married in such a prestigious family, but you are hell-bent on ruining it!' she took a deep breath and added, 'Tomorrow is your *Walima*. I won't be here to guide you. You better gather your wits and get ready on time for the function.' Both of them had a restless night and Bilquis left without even having her morning tea.

Maheen looked like a porcelain doll, sitting in the enormous tent on the silk *masnand*. Her red *Banarasi* suit was studded with gemstones, her long hair made in a neat bun. She carried herself with grace, welcoming all guests with *salaam*. Bilquis went to her and embraced her tightly. She then kissed her forehead. Sardara sat next to her on the *masnand*, looking pretty in a royal purple suit. She looked quizzically at her sister as if trying to read her thoughts. Bilquis heaved a sigh of relief. She had been talking animatedly to Maheen's mother-in-law when she sensed something amiss and turned to look at Maheen.

She had suddenly become very still, her head slumped backwards. A wave of panic went through Bilquis. She gently touched Maheen's shoulder. The young bride fell to the other side lifelessly.

Maheen's tragic end was a mystery to most people. As for Bilquis, she didn't have the inclination or time to grieve. She would have to immediately go on 'damage control' mode. Munnawar was devastated. He blamed himself for pushing Maheen to the brink. His little girl had not spoken to him much after her engagement, but he should have understood her fears, her dilemmas. Wasn't he the only one she confided in? Her sunken eyes, her whimpering whenever the subject of her marriage came up; he should have known! He should have protected her! Her weak heart could not take the pressure and she had quietly left without complaining. How could he forgive himself?

The rumours flying around in Ashraf's family were that the bride had eaten poison, that she did not want to get married in the first place, that she was not allowed to get married to the boy she loved and had ended her life! Some even felt that her mother, the daughter of a courtesan, had poisoned her! As soon as her daughter was buried, Bilquis dragged Munnawar to Ashraf's house to talk to the family. She did not feel any shame as Ashraf's mother accused her of knowingly marrying off her sick daughter to her son. Munnawar, however, lowered his head. With folded hands, he asked for their forgiveness. Bilquis gave him a steely glare. Then, clearing her throat, she offered her 12-year-old daughter, Sardara's hand in marriage to Ashraf. No one was prepared for this, least of all Munnawar. He almost collapsed when he heard his wife's words.

Before he could protest, Ashraf got up and took his hand. '*Main chu kabool*, I accept,' he said.

PART 2

Sardara was clear from the start that she would be staying in a separate wing in the palatial Shah Manzil. Ashraf, who had found Maheen too tongue-tied and docile, was delighted to see Sardara take a stand. She was yet to flower into a full-grown woman, but from her strength of character and her mesmerising beauty, it was clear that very soon, she would turn into someone to reckon with. Ashraf had led a protected life because of his illness, without anyone who he could call a friend. He did not protest when his mother-in-law moved in and stayed with Sardara, sleeping in her room and fiercely guarding her.

Munnawar became a recluse after Maheen's death. He shut himself in his room, with only the servants enquiring about him from time to time. One stormy morning, the telephone in Sardara's room rang. Bilquis heard from one of the servants that Munnawar was no more. He had died in a fire. Paradise House had been razed to the ground. In her heart, Bilquis knew that her husband had deliberately started the fire.

Jaleel assured Bilquis that he would take stock of Munnawar's business. He visited his sister every day to console her. Bilquis had decided to stay with Sardara till the time her house would be rebuilt. A month later, Jaleel gave her the news that not a penny remained in her name. 'Munnawar was in heavy debt. He had taken a huge loan from the bank too. All his assets and businesses will be evaluated and auctioned to repay the bank,' he told his shocked sister. Bilquis demanded to see the lawyers. She carefully went through all the paperwork. There wasn't much that she could do. She suspected Jaleel's hand in the fraud, but couldn't prove anything. She let go of the ties with her brother and his family, and any connection with her past.

Ashraf's infatuation with his wife grew by the day. He had already shown her a plot where they would have a house of their own. He indulged in Sardara's every whim and fancy. It was a difficult task indeed because Sardara was hard to please. It took two years to build her dream home. In the end, Ashraf too had to agree that she had great taste. She had surely been advised by Bilquis. Nevertheless, every detail of the new mansion was looked into. It looked like a museum with artefacts brought from around the world, but it was predominantly Kashmiri in nature, with *khatamband* ceilings made from individual carved wooden tiles to *papier mache* doors and windows painted in pure gold and silver. Persian silk carpets lined the floor as well as the curved stairway that emerged from the large drawing room and went right up to the second-floor lobby. One of Sardara's favourite rooms was the *'ittar room'* which had dozens of cutglass canisters of all shapes and sizes placed on marble pedestals that contained perfumes handpicked from all over the world. Expensive chandeliers graced the ceilings. The massive kitchen had the most modern gadgets shipped from Europe. The layout of the terraced garden would put any Mughal garden to shame. Cherry, apple, apricot, pear and plum trees thrived in the backyard. Sardara presided over her palace like a queen.

Ashraf never did see why his parents and sisters taunted him about being henpecked. He had met them on occasions like Eid or a relative's wedding, and they always managed to corner him with accusations of being forced to ignore his own family. He knew things had gone too far when on one such occasion, his mother beat her breasts and wailed, '*Tami daeni te tamsinzi maaji khuv muan nechuv*, that witch and her mother have eaten my son.' He refused to step inside his mother's house after that day.

Fifteen years after his marriage to Sardara, a massive epileptic fit followed by a heart attack killed Ashraf. Sardara, who was not yet 30, was left to fend for her three young children and an ageing garrulous mother. Everything she had ever asked for in life till then, had been offered to her on a platter. But now, the struggle that lay ahead was like climbing Everest. She was completely shunned and disowned by Ashraf's family. Not that she was inclined to reach out to them. Her pride did not allow that.

'I will kill my kids and myself, but never beg from them,' she told her mother.

With her chin high, she continued to live the lavish life she was used to. The servants, gardeners and drivers remained at her disposal until they themselves discreetly left one by one, as they realised that she was unable to pay their salaries.

PART 3

Nazneen constantly lived in the shadow of her elder sister Asifa. Their mother, Sardara, who they called Mauji, was short-tempered and demanded them to be perfectly turned out. She could not suffer fools. So, they obeyed her, but sometimes, Nazneen would get into trouble. It was then that Asifa would protect her and take the blame. The mother was a control freak when it came to her daughters, but she discovered soon enough that she did not have a hold over her son, Tariq, the youngest born. He was spoilt, irresponsible and brash. While his sisters graduated with honours, he barely managed to scrape through school. He was still in his teens when his mother caught him taking drugs. He found ways to hide bottles of alcohol in his room, but Sardara would always sniff them out. There were times when she, at the behest of Bilquis, beat him up with nettle stalks, shut him in his room or simply refused to serve him food. Yet, he remained incorrigible.

Asifa inherited her mother's stunning good looks. She was tall and slim. Golden lashes swept her aquamarine eyes. Light brown hair, neatly braided with a puff above her forehead, that would become her trademark style, almost touched her knees. Dimpled cheeks, a strong chin that gave a hint of arrogance and a shapely nose with a single studded nose pin, made many a young man weak in his knees. Nazneen, on the other hand, lacked the poise of her elder sister. Clumsy and nervous, she would never be seen without her sister by her side. But she had been bestowed with the most extraordinary brown eyes that lit up when she smiled. It was probably that bewitching smile which captured the heart of her young and dashing neighbour, Abrar.

What started as an innocent interaction one spring evening between Abrar and Nazneen, turned into a full-blown love affair before autumn arrived. Abrar, the scion of the notorious Lone family, had never got a chance to talk to Nazneen till the night she figured out a flashlight code that he had invented. As Nazneen sat by her desk to study, her eyes were drawn to the blinking of a light coming from the attic of the opposite house. This had happened before too, but she hadn't paid much attention. This time, her interest was piqued because she had seen the figure of the boy, the one she had a crush on, enter the room. Soon, he switched off the light and started flashing the torch in her direction. Mesmerised, she watched intently. There was a pattern to the way the lights were flickering. She started writing the order in her notebook. It took her an hour to understand the alphabets coinciding with the flickering lights. She laughed aloud. It was her turn to switch off the light in her room. With the help of her table lamp, she sent him a message, 'Smart,' to which he replied, 'ha, ha, ha.'

Nazneen's world had changed overnight. The days suddenly seemed too long, studies boring and her elder sister irritating. All she wanted to do was get a glimpse of the handsome young man who was the first one ever to show some interest in her. His messages had become bolder with time. Finally, she could overcome the complex of the '*medher shakal*, plain Jane' tag, one that had constantly demoralized her. Not a day passed before someone commented how wilted she looked when compared to her sister. Being herself – carefree, and whimsical – was a liberating feeling for Nazneen. This wouldn't have happened if she hadn't met Abrar. Their first secret rendezvous lasted just 15 minutes when she hurriedly hopped into a *shikara*, a tiny boat, at Nehru Park which he had hired especially for her. She sat uncomfortably resting her back against the bolster, her long legs stretching across the sofa, her feet gently touching his knee as he sat right opposite her. She placed her hand on her chest as if to slow down her heart which was beating so fast. It scared her. He too looked around nervously, perspiring even as the chilly breeze blew across his handsome face. Both felt shy. There was hardly any eye contact. But the smiles were there, and they said a million things to each other without speaking.

They met a few times before Nazneen's secret reached the ears of her mother. Sardara had been an enigma in the neighbourhood where her husband had built the palatial house for her. Her legend grew, thanks to the free promotion by all those who had known her or had heard of her. A ravishing beauty who held the heart of her husband even as a child bride, the manner in which she threw out her mother-in-law (*nari kor nas thap te nyabar chakken*, she got hold of her arm and dragged her out of the house), her trunk load of expensive jewellery, her fine costumes that cost millions, all these stories about her, obviously peppered to make them colourful, were told and retold by idle housewives and frustrated men.

However, since her husband's death, she was rarely seen outside her house. On one occasion when her uncle Jaleel had begged Bilquis and her to attend his daughter's *nikah* ceremony, she was seen sitting aloof, wearing a cream-coloured hand embroidered suit, her head covered with a *mukhash* dupatta. But the women had gossiped about how she refused to eat with anyone else in a *trami*, hardly touching the food she was offered separately.

'*Takbur kya chus*, what pride she has,' they whispered, not missing her arched eyebrows and the way she sat with her head held high. She had gifted the bride a gold necklace set with diamonds and rubies. Sardara had fought hard to keep up her reputation as a wealthy *khandani* woman.

The sky seemed to have fallen on her head when she heard that Nazneen had been meeting the fellow from the family next door. She had loathed the Lones, who, no doubt, were a wealthy and powerful family, but whose business seemed to be dubious. She suspected that they were smugglers, or probably, dealt in narcotics. Sardara knew the reason why all her maternal relatives were kept under a shroud of secrecy by her mother. By marrying her father, Bilquis had left her infamous background far behind and there was no way Sardara would allow anything to erode the well-constructed façade.

Hot tears of frustration fell down Nazneen's flushed cheeks as Mauji kept slapping her, even as her hand hurt. She then pulled her hair and dragged her to one corner of her room.

'*Zahar dimai agar beya amis shiksiyas samkhak*, I'll poison you if you meet that pauper again,' she yelled, wagging her finger at the terrified Nazneen.

Bilquis looked on, with a big frown on her face, while her brother Tariq excitedly talked about the Lone boys, calling them 'smugglers' and 'thieves.' Asifa, who was equally angry, especially since she had no clue about her sister's romance, asked her from where she got the guts to do something so daring! Nazneen looked at her defiantly. Wiping her face with her dupatta, she climbed into her bed and went off to sleep. She did not step outside her room for the next few days. One morning, she was gone before anyone else woke up for morning prayers.

Nazneen found a huge support in her grand uncle Jaleel and to her surprise, his wife, Zainab.

'There is no way your mother will agree to marry you off in the *Lone khandan, beti*. There is no point in informing her. If Abrar is willing, the *baraat* can go from my house,' he said in a consoling voice.

Zainab hugged her as she wept on her shoulder. Zainab had not forgotten the insults Bilquis had hurled at her family after Jaleel took over the family business. Sardara too had behaved at her daughter's wedding as if she was doing them a favour by attending the functions. In her heart, Zainab was thrilled about the scandal that would follow Nazneen's wedding. It would leave a permanent scar of shame on Bilquis and Sardara, she felt with a sense of satisfaction.

Abrar and Nazneen got married at Jaleel's house in a small ceremony with just the groom's elder brother and father accompanying him. Nazneen wore a dress borrowed from Jaleel's daughter. Abrar gave her a gold necklace and ring, the only ornaments she wore when she left for her new home. She was desperate to see her mother. She hoped that she would be forgiven. No matter how much she tried to contact her family, there was complete silence from them. One day she mustered enough courage to ring their doorbell. Her sister came hurriedly out and whispered to her that she was dead to the family and she should never try to talk to them again.

'We will pray for your soul, Nazneen,' she said emotionlessly.

Nazneen looked for a long time at the majestic gate that was permanently shut for her. The distance between the two homes had grown by thousands of miles overnight.

Sardara did not shed a tear when Nazneen left.

'*Meya chat tumsinz rag*, I have cut the vein that bonded us,' said Bilquis to her, urging her to do the same.

'Yes, it's better to sever off the arm that has developed gangrene,' she replied, vehemently shaking her head.

PART 4

It was a chilly autumn evening when the mother-daughter duo sat on the threadbare carpet in the *hamaan* room that clearly had seen better days. Heated with burning coals or firewood underneath the cemented floor, the room was cosy in the cold Srinagar winters where temperatures sometimes dipped well beyond minus. But that day, it was freezing there, as the shed used as a store for wood and coal remained empty. Dressed in heavy woollen *pherans*, their heads covered in scarves and feet in mismatched socks, Sardara and her mother, Bilquis, talked about the days gone by.

'Muzzafar was gutless; he buckled under pressure when his daughter died,' Bilquis said. 'He blamed me for the death of his sick daughter!' she lamented.

Sardara took a long puff of the hookah and passed it to her mother with a sigh. She gave out a bitter laugh, remembering her own husband. 'Ashraf thought he could control me! What good was he anyway? I had a separate bedroom after Tariq was born!' she said giggling, 'He was so thin and sickly, I was afraid he would die in my bed. I worried how I could sleep in the same bed as a dead body!'

The bare walls echoed their laughter.

'Jaleel was the biggest disappointment, a serpent,' Bilquis said, remembering the time when her brother had licked his lips when she was signing off her entire business to him.

'And Tariq, where is your beloved son these days?' she mocked Sardara.

'Must be dead in some dirty drain; don't talk about him ever,' she replied. 'Remember how he came a couple of years ago asking for his share of the property? Well, it felt so nice when he went around from room to room finding them empty. He couldn't believe that I had sold off the furniture, the wall hangings and the chandeliers. Where was I supposed to get the money for the luxurious life he was used to? Bloody ignorant fool! He has not worked for a single day in his life and expects to be treated like a king! So, I threw him out,' Sardara fumed. 'In any case, what was the point of educating the three of them?' she said, referring to her children. 'Asifa remains a slave to her husband, who, I hear, writes poetry. I was told he has no qualms about reciting the ones he has written about her in public. Imagine! Somebody tell him his poetry will not feed them and their brood! It's good that we don't see them often.'

Bilquis giggled as she remembered the time when once on Eid, just after lunch, Asifa's husband stood up even when all of them were still sitting on the *dastarkhwan* and started reciting a poem about the sheep that had been slaughtered during *qurbani*. Everyone had been dumbstruck while Bilquis and Sardara had sniggered at him. Asifa had vowed never again to bring her family to visit her mother and grandmother. They tried to remember the poem that Asif read. The '*mujwoonth*' the nickname they had for Asifa's husband, who was often awkward and shabbily dressed, looked far from the scholar that he was portrayed as, sounded more like a *khar*, a donkey, they agreed.

Raising both hands towards the heavens, Sardara said, 'Allah, please don't give anyone a daughter like Nazneen! Who would have thought that the innocent-looking girl would turn out to be such a wench! She is the reason for our grief!'

Bilquis wholeheartedly agreed with her. 'She was such a bright student. She could have worked and looked after us, but she could not control her youth and eloped with the first man who came her way!'

As the night grew colder, they huddled together in a bed they shared which was covered with a thin mattress and three dust-laden quilts. Sipping salty tea in chipped porcelain cups, they spent the rest of the night chatting, laughing and mocking the rest of the world for which they were long dead.

THE END

Glossary

Tumbakhnari	–	A musical instrument in the shape of a drum, cast in a clay funnel like case
Manzimuour	–	The matchmaker
Khandaan	–	Clan
Kehwa	–	Kashmiri tea made with condiments, saffron and special tea leaves
Mehendi	–	Henna
Khatirdaari	–	Hospitality
Aashiq	–	Lover
Rishta	–	Matrimonial alliance
Basrakh	–	A sweet made from flour and powdered sugar
Chula	–	Oven
Waza	–	Cook
Jumka	–	Long, dangling earrings
Nikaah	–	Islamic marriage contract
Harissa	–	A mutton-based delicacy served in winters

Glossary

Jajeer	–	Hookah, pipe for smoking tobacco
Kangri	–	A clay pot filled with lighted charcoal which can be carried by a person; used to keep oneself warm
Pheran	–	A long loose upper garment worn especially in winters
Jinn	–	(In Arabian and Muslim mythology) An intelligent spirit of lower rank than the angels, able to appear in human and animal forms and to possess humans
Jannat	–	Paradise
Lanchekot	–	A slanderous word to describe a eunuch
Ruksati	–	The ceremony when the bride leaves for her matrimonial home
Walima	–	Reception
Lanch	–	Transgender
Dastarkhwan	–	A cloth spread on the floor on which food is served
Kandur	–	Baker
Nun chai	–	Pink salty tea
Shukr Alhamdullilah	–	Thank Allah
Sharara	–	A traditional dress

Glossary

Bakarkhani	–	A flaky type of bread
Karakuli	–	A special lambskin cap
Wanwun	–	Traditional singing
Tabak maaz	–	A dish made of lamb ribs
Masnand	–	A carpet laid out for the bride and groom.
Ittar	–	Perfume

Printed in Dunstable, United Kingdom